THE WINE OF LIFE

THE WINE OF LIFE

LESLEY EGAN

DOUBLEDAY & COMPANY, INC.
GARDEN CITY, NEW YORK

All of the characters in this book
are fictitious, and any resemblance
to actual persons, living or dead,
is purely coincidental.

This one is for Margaret

There's nothing serious in mortality—
All is but toys; renown and grace is dead,
The wine of life is drawn, and the mere lees
Is left this vault to brag of.
—*Macbeth*, Act 2, Scene 3

Men have died from time to time, and worms
Have eaten them, but not for love.
—*As You Like It*, Act 4, Scene 1

THE WINE OF LIFE

CHAPTER ONE

William De Witt had dropped by the office to take Jesse out to lunch. As the head of the Western Association for Psychic Research, De Witt had roped Jesse in as treasurer; not that there was much work in it. Over the last couple of months, he had been engaged, with his little crew of psychics, in a triangular experiment aimed at getting the cross-correspondence communications with his own team of psychics, a group at Maimonides Medical Center in New York, and another group at Durham University.

Jesse listened to his enthusiastic testimony with small interest. The evidential communications had been coming through, but it was the kind of cross correspondence, from a variety of accredited psychics, that had been coming through to a number of parapsychological researchers for the last ninety years—evidential, but monotonous and fairly boring.

He said as he finished his coffee, "I can't stay to gossip, William—I've got a two o'clock appointment."

"Oh well, I just thought you'd be interested in the latest evidence." They went out to the parking lot, and Jesse fished for his keys as they came up to the Mercedes sedan. De Witt began suddenly to laugh, and leaned up against the car, as long and lanky and dark as Jesse, laughing. "Just a minute—I haven't told you about Charles' latest hit."

"Oh?" Jesse paused. Charles MacDonald was one of De Witt's team of psychics; he was a gifted psychometrist, but his psychic pronouncements were often rather cryptic, needing some interpretation.

De Witt chuckled. "Rather silly," he said, "but interesting. This woman came to him for a reading a couple of weeks ago. Gave him a man's ring to hold. All she said was, she was having trouble with her husband and could he tell her anything. He told her yes, he got the definite impression that all her trouble was caused by Moonrose Mischief III and Penhallow's Minuet of Moonrose."

Jesse laughed. "Outlandish even for Charles."

"Say it twice," said De Witt amusedly. "The woman thought he was kidding her—making up something—went away in a huff. But last week she came in to apologize and say he'd been absolutely right. Turns out her husband is a professional dog handler—you know, shows dogs for the owners. And those dogs—Moonrose Mischief and the other one—are prize-winning cocker spaniels he's been showing for a wealthy socialite female. In the course of which they've started a hot and heavy affair, and he's now asked his wife for a divorce and is all set to marry the wealthy socialite."

Jesse laughed. "That is a funny one—Charles right again, if in a roundabout way. I've got to run, William—this appointment."

In fact, he was late getting back to the office in the highrise building on Wilshire Boulevard. When he came in, he found the new client waiting for him under the eyes of his twin blond secretaries Jean and Jamesina Gordon, and apologized for being late.

"I was a little early," said the client amiably.

"Mr. Kinsolving? Come into my office and tell me what I can do for you."

Kinsolving had called to make an appointment a few days earlier. He followed Jesse into the inner office and accepted the chair beside the desk. He was a man of middle height, thin and casually well tailored in a gray business suit, white shirt, discreet tie. You'd look at him twice, thought Jesse, to realize that he was a rather handsome man, with regular clean-cut features, intelligent blue eyes under heavy brows, his dark hair still plentiful in a severe short cut.

He said, "It's nothing very important, Mr. Falkenstein. I just want to make a will." He had an attractive one-sided smile. "Here I'm always advising my clients to make wills like sensible people, and I only get around to it myself now. And of course, we have dealings with several attorneys with the firm, but I just thought—for personal business—I'd go to someone outside, as it were." He smiled again. "My sister accuses me of being secretive, but I don't think I am—only cautious."

"Just as well," said Jesse.

"Well, Mrs. Gorman had mentioned your name," said Kinsolving.

"Oh, I see." Mrs. Gorman was a longtime client; she conceived a new codicil to her will on the average of once every three months, and it was now a respectably lengthy document.

Kinsolving laughed. "The nice, silly, sentimental woman," he said. "Fortunately she has just enough sense to realize she doesn't know anything about money, and leaves it all up to me. She's so devoted to those dogs of hers."

Jesse laughed. "The dear lady is nervous about my office décor." He glanced up at the one large picture in its heavy oak frame on the wall behind the desk.

Kinsolving's eyes followed his and surprisingly he recognized it at once. "That's a very nice Holbein reproduction. Oh, yes, Sir Thomas More. Well, he is rather a grim-looking old boy, isn't he?"

"Very upright man of integrity," said Jesse. "Very sound lawyer."

"Until he made the mistake of getting into a religious argument with Henry VIII," said Kinsolving with a grin. "Mrs. Gorman and her dogs—well, it'd be nice to have a pet—I like cats—but in my position it'd be impossible. I'm away all day, and sometimes I have to travel for the firm. Mrs. Gorman mentioned that you have a mastiff."

"For our sins. My wife acquired him under the misapprehension that he was a Boxer, and then he kept growing—"

Kinsolving laughed. "Well, I won't take up much of your time, Mr. Falkenstein—it's a very simple will. I've got a forty-second birthday coming up in November, and it's past time I made a will." He had a briefcase on his lap; he opened it and took out a single sheet of paper. "I've just noted down what the estate consists of." He passed it over—he had a copperplate handwriting nearly as neat as Jesse's own. "I'd better tell you something of my circumstances."

He was a tax specialist with an old and prestigious brokerage firm. For a man of his age he had amassed quite a nice estate; Jesse read him as a very shrewd businessman, and of course his job was the knowledge of how to protect investments from the ravages of the income tax. He owned the condominium where he lived clear; he said he'd had a windfall several years ago and thought that a sound investment. It was a good address, in upper Hollywood; it would represent a value of about two hundred thousand, and in addition he had not inconsiderable holdings in money market funds, a fiduciary trust.

"It's all to go to my sister," he said. "Mrs. Shirley Grant."

"There aren't any other relatives?"

"Well, no, not to speak of." Kinsolving sat back in the chair and passed a manicured hand over his mouth. "You see, Mr. Falkenstein, sixteen years ago I was engaged to be married. I think Marion and I would have been very happy together—we wanted a family—and my life would have taken a different direction, you can say. But she was killed by a hit-run driver two days before the wedding—and, well, since then I simply haven't met a woman I could feel that deeply about. I expect you could say I've just—vegetated. Gone on alone. I expect I got in a rut—I suppose some people would say I live a dull life, but I don't know. I get to feeling a little depressed sometimes, thinking of all I've missed in life, but on the whole I go along all right. I enjoy my work, I'm interested in that, and I get in some golf, and I've got a friend, a client, Sam Ulrich, who gives me a game of chess now and then, and I like to read, and listen to music. I do all right. Well—this will. By the way, I've got a safe at the apartment— easier than renting a safety-deposit box—I expect you'd better have the combination."

He wanted to leave everything to his sister, Mrs. Shirley Grant. "Our parents are gone. Dad died five years ago, and Mother a couple of years later. Alan's a very nice fellow," he added, "he's been a good husband to Shirley, but he'll never be a money-maker. The only thing is, I can't give you a permanent address, not now. Alan's been teaching at Hollywood High School since they've been married, but he's moving up a step now— he'll be teaching at the university at Santa Barbara starting in September, he's got a pretty good contract there. They'll be moving up there, they've got the house here up for sale, but you know real estate isn't moving very fast—the interest rates. It may be that Alan will have to go up there and get a temporary apartment until the house here is sold and through es- crow. Of course, they'd like to get up there, moved into another house, by the beginning of the school year—the kids are thirteen and eleven—but it may not work out. I'll give you the current address." It was Oporto Drive. "As soon as they've moved, I'll let you know the new address."

"There aren't any other relatives? It may be advisable to exclude them with a token legacy."

"One dollar to prevent challenging the will?" Kinsolving laughed. "Oh, I don't think so—there are cousins, second cousins, but Shirley and I haven't kept up with them at all—they all live up north, I think. And there's Aunt Janet, Mrs. Janet Culver. My father's youngest sister. She and her husband never had any children. They lived in Chicago, and when he died about five years ago, she came back to California, she was tired of the winters in Illinois. But her husband left her a very good annuity, she's all right, and besides she's about seventy-five. I really don't expect to die for quite some time, you just have to be—foresighted. Make sensible plans."

"Yes, that's only sensible."

"Shirley and Alan have made mutual wills—everything to each other— and left me as guardian in case they both die while the children are still minors. That isn't very likely, of course, but you never know."

"Well, we'll get this drawn up for you, Mr. Kinsolving, probably by the end of the week."

"That's fine. I'll be glad to have it done and off my mind—shouldn't have put it off," said Kinsolving. He stood up and gave Jesse his attractive one-sided smile. "I'll be relieved to have it taken care of."

"We'll let you know when you can come in and sign it," said Jesse.

"Fine. You can get me at the office or at home." He offered his hand. "Thanks very much, Mr. Falkenstein. You'll be in touch then?"

"In a few days."

"Fine." Kinsolving went out, and in the door to the anteroom Jimmy Gordon said expressionlessly, "Mrs. Cochran is here, Mr. Falkenstein."

Jesse suppressed a few forcible words. Mrs. Cochran had somewhat more money and less sense than she should have had, and at the moment was bent on instituting a lawsuit against a large department store on the grounds that one of its clerks had insulted her over an argument about bathing suit sizes. It was going to take quite a lot of persuasion to convince her that it would be a useless legal exercise.

He had two divorce hearings tomorrow, and sometime next week the hearing would get underway on the litigation about the deed to an empty lot in Glendale, which could be time-consuming and confusing—two cousins of the same name claiming it, and a mutual uncle's will not specifying which. Wills, however meticulously drawn, could sometimes be unspecific.

He got rid of Mrs. Cochran within half an hour and settled to draft Robert Kinsolving's will in his finicky copperplate handwriting; he dictated it to Jean before he left the office.

"I don't know when I'll get to it, Mr. Falkenstein—there's that Fielding contract, and all the paperwork on the Brunson divorce—"

"No particular hurry," said Jesse. Kinsolving—whom he liked, a good man, an attractive man—wasn't about to drop dead tomorrow. Just being foresighted.

He spent a tiresome day in court on Wednesday. In the third week of July, the usual summer heat wave in Southern California was getting underway. Of course, the Central Criminal Courthouse was air-conditioned, and so was the Mercedes, but the underground parking lot wasn't —it was like the anteroom of hell, and the air-conditioning didn't get the car cooled off until Jesse got home.

On Thursday he was peacefully proofreading a contract between a building contractor and a major investor when he had an unexpected call from a little-known client—he'd once drawn a will for the man a year or so ago—who was incarcerated in the county jail on a charge of assault, and screaming for help. Jesse turned the contract over to Jean, drove down to the jail, and discovered that it was a tempest in a teapot—the client's girlfriend had accused him of attempted rape on rather flimsy evidence.

"Listen," said the client morosely, "I was drunk—we was both kind of drunk—I don't figure I could have done it even if I'd meant to, see. She was just mad at me because I'd forgot to get her a birthday present." He was fifty-eight and twice divorced; the girlfriend was sixty, with a small record of petty theft.

Jesse arranged for bail; the man would probably be arraigned within a few days. It would cost some time in court in a couple of weeks' time, but he could probably get the charge dismissed. People! he thought, driving home. The heat had built up more; when it arrived this early, it was going to be a bad summer. And why one of the world's greatest cities had grown up in this climate was just one of those mysteries. And thank God for air-conditioning.

He had to be in court on Friday afternoon for another divorce hearing. He got back to the office about three-thirty; he had an appointment with a woman who wanted a divorce, and listened to a long list of grievances. People, he thought again. The woman was a raddled harridan, the husband apparently a drunk and a chaser, and there wasn't much to choose between them. He got all the relevant details, she grudgingly parted with a retainer, and he saw her out with relief. It was getting on to four-thirty.

"Oh, I've got that Kinsolving will copied," said Jimmy in the door of his office.

"Good." It was, of course, a short and simple will. He proofread it—as usual, the copy was crisp and correct. He wondered now and then what on earth he would do if a couple of personable young men should rob him of his efficient and excellent twin Gordons; they were, after all, extremely pretty girls, brown-eyed blondes with eye-catching figures. He wouldn't find one such efficient secretary in a hurry, let alone two.

It was five o'clock when he called Robert Kinsolving at the brokerage firm. "Oh, you just caught me leaving," said Kinsolving.

"Your will's all ready to be signed, you can come in anytime."

"Oh, fine," said Kinsolving amiably. "Be just as happy to have it done and off my mind. I don't suppose you keep office hours on the weekend."

"Any time on Monday," said Jesse.

"Well, let's see, I've got an appointment in the morning—and I've got to talk to that trustee on the Clymer business, but I can put that off until late afternoon. I'll tell you," said Kinsolving, "I'll drop by about two on Monday afternoon to sign it. That all right? I suppose your girls can act as witnesses."

"Yes, that'll be fine. You can leave it with me—I've got all the rest of the relevant paperwork. I'll see you then."

And thank God not only for air-conditioning but for the weekend. It was good to get home, to the sprawling big two-story house at the end of Paradise Lane off Coldwater Canyon Drive. At this time of year it wasn't dark yet, the front lights not on, but the gate was open, which meant that Athelstane was in. He stopped to close the gates behind him, drove into the garage and parked the Mercedes beside Nell's identical sedan, and went in the back door. The central air-conditioning was on, and damn what it cost. Nell was stretched out on the couch in the living room reading, and looked up in surprise. "You're early—" She scrambled up to kiss him, his lovely Nell with her bright brown hair in its fat chignon, but these days not exactly her usual slim self. The new baby had got started in March and was due in November; they both hoped it would be a girl. Davy came running up, discovering that Daddy was home; at just over two years he was more energetic and voluble by the day.

"Daddy read—read about Dame Wiggins!" He had lately been introduced to Dame Wiggins and her wonderful cats in the new nursery book.

"Later," said Jesse. "You all right?"

"Never better," said Nell. "Being pregnant agrees with me." Athelstane, the huge brindle mastiff, was sprawled on the hearthrug before the empty fireplace, and the arrogant liquid length of Murteza, the royal Siamese, was in his favorite place on the mantel.

"Dame Wiggins!" insisted Davy.

"I can offer you steak and French fries, or cold cuts and potato salad. What sort of a day did you have?"

"Middling," said Jesse. "I'll have the steak. But I need a long drink first." He sat down in his armchair, and Davy clambered up to his lap clutching the big book of nursery rhymes. "Oh, all right, boy, we'll find Dame Wiggins."

Nell brought him a tall bourbon and soda, and a glass of Dubonnet for herself. "Fran and Andrew are coming to dinner on Monday night. I called your father too, but he's got to be in Sacramento for the firm." Falkenstein Senior was a busy corporation attorney.

"Um," said Jesse, sampling his drink gratefully.

There was paperwork he could be doing at the office, and sometime he would have to get back to the Huff woman's attorney about that divorce settlement; he was representing Huff, and if the other attorney prevailed,

Huff was going to get a raw deal. The woman was a mercenary slut, out for all she could get. But he was damned if he'd do overtime on the weekend.

He stayed in with Davy while Nell went out marketing on Saturday morning. She came home with an armful of library books as well. "Talk about luck," she said, dumping them down on the coffee table when she had put the groceries away. "I wasn't even sure any library would have it —it's a British publication—but I asked just on the chance, and they had it and it was in. That new book of Keith Simpson's, *Forty Years of Murder.* You know, he's the great forensic specialist for Scotland Yard." Nell was a true-crime buff.

"Um," said Jesse, who was somnolently rereading *The Daughter of Time* while Davy sprawled across the living room floor chattering at a stuffed cat.

"And I've definitely decided," added Nell, "either Esther or Judith."

"It's probably another boy."

"Oh, don't be negative, Jesse. I'm positively certain sure it's a girl. Esther or Judith—or just possibly Sarah."

"Just in case, we'd better decide on the alternative."

"Oh well, I wouldn't be too particular—Daniel or Matthew or even Adam," said Nell largely. "But I know it's a girl."

Jesse looked up at her fondly and said, "Women. You can't know."

"Well, I do. And I'm going to spend the rest of the day with Dr. Simpson—except that I want to call Fran to ask what she did about the kitchen curtains."

Not altogether unexpectedly, on Sunday afternoon he had a call from a doctor at Cedars-Sinai Medical Center who told him that Clifford Dawson had just died. "You were listed as the one to notify," said the doctor rather indifferently.

"Oh, yes—thanks very much." And that would entail a little more work —and paperwork. Dawson had been an elderly recluse, and there were no relatives; he had left all his assets to charity, and had been terminally ill with emphysema for some time. The most immediate thing was to arrange a funeral; Jesse called a mortician and arranged for the body to be picked up. At least he didn't have to be in court tomorrow.

But Monday turned out to be one of those trying days. He spent a while on the phone that morning talking to someone in the trust department of a local bank about the Dawson estate; it would have to be administered by the bank until the will was through probate. Then Mrs. Huff's attorney called him, and they spent an hour arguing about the divorce settlement.

"I must refuse absolutely to meet your suggestions," said the other attorney several times over. "My client has been very shabbily treated by her husband, and it will be easy enough to show that he has locked her out of their joint property, cut off all funds for her living expenses, and used gross and profane language to her. She will certainly refuse to settle for less than the half million she is asking, and title to the property, which I can only regard as eminently fair under the circumstances. And I must say, Mr. Falkenstein—"

"And I must say," said Jesse, goaded at last into some plain speaking, "that it would be equally easy for me to show in court that your client is promiscuous, a part-time lush and an evil-tempered harridan whose behavior to the man forced him to kick her out of the house and refuse her any more money for liquor and shopping sprees. Over the dozen years they've been married, she's cost him one hell of a bundle, and God knows he hasn't got much for it. I'll tell you, I'm not about to see him taken for any more. We're offering her the house and the car, and that's it. You can take it or leave it."

The other man spluttered and argued, but Jesse had had enough of him. He was feeling annoyed as he put down the phone. And then Jimmy Gordon ushered in a Mrs. O'Reilly who was fat, in her forties and unsuitably dressed in a baby-blue ruffled sundress, and she wanted to instigate a lawsuit against Buffum's Department Store.

"I'm sure you'll agree with me that I certainly have a case, I've never been so insulted in my life—I'm an honest, respectable woman, I can bring all sorts of character witnesses to say so—and of course I apologized at once, I simply don't know how it could have happened, I am a little absentminded sometimes, but to call me a thief and arrest me—well, I've just never been so insulted! I'd been doing quite a lot of shopping, I had my niece's birthday to think about, and we're making a trip east to visit my husband's brother next month, I was looking for some new dresses and shoes—and it's such a nuisance to have stores send things, they say tomorrow and you don't get them delivered for days—terrible inefficiency—and so I did have several packages with me, and naturally I took them into the dressing room with me, what with all the thieves around, even in good stores—I was simply trying on a few dresses, and I just can't think how that one came to get into the bag from the Broadway—I'd got my niece a very nice housecoat, it was on sale too—I'm certainly not a thief! I was never so insulted when that—that woman came up as I was leaving and rummaged through all my parcels—of course I apologized right away when that dress showed up, I can't think how it came to be there, but to have me arrested—I had to call my husband, and those awful policemen looking at me—"

Jesse managed to stem the flow and got a few answers to questions. No, they hadn't actually charged her, the detective at the store and the police had just warned her, but it was plain they all thought she was a thief and she had never been so insulted. She was going to sue that store for slander or libel or something, and get damages, a lot of money for the way she'd been insulted.

Wearily Jesse spelled it out for her that she didn't really have a case and had better forget it. She told him he was a pretty poor excuse for a lawyer, and that he'd better not try to charge her for professional advice when that was all he had to say to her. She marched out indignantly, and Jesse started out for a belated lunch.

He got back at two o'clock, in time to take a call from Huff, whose backbone had finally been stiffened by repeated threats and demands from his wife, and he was now refusing to offer her any settlement at all. "I'll be damned if she gets a dime, and that's my last word. Look, I can get in ahead of her and divorce her, can't I? For desertion or something? Then she couldn't ask for a settlement at all, could she? Look, she did walk out of the house—after the argument we had about that bill for that jewelry— I told you about that, the time she threw the lamp at me and damn near brained me. I'll be damned if she gets another dime—"

Jesse talked to him for half an hour. What with all they could show in court about Mrs. Huff's record, he doubted that she'd get much of a settlement. Huff had better stay quiet and let the house go, if the judge wanted to give it to her, and count himself lucky to get out of it.

At least he hadn't any more appointments this afternoon. There was paperwork to do on the Dawson thing; but as he started to think about that, Jean looked in the door and said, "That Mr. Kinsolving hasn't shown up, Mr. Falkenstein. He was supposed to come in to sign his will at two o'clock."

Jesse felt a little surprised. Kinsolving had struck him as a man who would be punctual about keeping appointments, or call in with some reasonable excuse. Well, he may have been delayed. It was just after three. He said, "You'd better try to get him at his office—he may have forgotten. It's Harlow and Wolfe." It wasn't very important; Kinsolving would come in sometime.

Jean came back five minutes later and said, "He isn't in the office, but they say that isn't unusual, he isn't in all day every day."

"And I don't suppose he'll be home until after six."

"I left a message for him to call."

"All we can do. All right, try to reach him again first thing in the morning." Jesse called the mortician again, got the final figure on the funeral cost, called the trust officer at the bank. Tomorrow or next day he'd have to set up that account with the trust department, pending the probate of the will; there wasn't much hurry.

He left the office a little early and was glad to go. Outside the building, in the blacktopped parking lot, the heat had built up some more. It was nothing to what they would get a couple of months from now, but bad enough. Later on the humidity would rise too. He switched on the air-conditioning in the Mercedes; the home-going traffic was already thick, and he had to wait for two changes of the light at the intersection to turn off at La Brea.

He came in the back door to find Nell putting the finishing touches to a big bowl of salad. "Fran and Andrew will be here any minute. Reasonably good day, darling?"

"My Lord, what a day," said Jesse. "That O'Reilly woman— Oh well, take it as it comes." Davy was crawling around the floor with a toy airplane, making the appropriate loud noises. "I need a drink, but I suppose I'd better wait for Andrew." He wandered into the living room. Athelstane was sound asleep on the hearthrug, the elegant Murteza curled up against his great chest purring.

They both woke up five minutes later when the Clocks arrived, coming in the back door without announcement. Jesse's little sister Fran was again her slim svelte self dark and vivacious, with the baby now six months old. "Everything's in the oven," said Nell, "we can sit down and have a quiet drink before dinner." Fran had already got the bottle of Dubonnet out of the refrigerator. Since a month ago baby Elaine had ceased to depend on her mother for feeding, so Fran was freer to come and go; and they had found a motherly babysitter across the street.

Sergeant Andrew Clock, LAPD, Hollywood Division, was not as well turned out as Fran. His prognathous jaw needed a shave, his suit was rumpled, his tie crooked, and he looked tired. He collapsed onto the couch, pulled his tie loose, and said, "I could stand a drink."

"I was just waiting for you."

Davy clambered into Clock's lap and said distinctly, "Unka."

"There, he's almost got it," said Clock. "Uncle, Davy."

"Unka!"

Nell and Fran came in and sat down with glasses of Dubonnet, which they had both expensively adopted. "We'll get him off to bed before we have dinner," said Nell. "He's already had supper." Jesse went out to the kitchen and built two hefty bourbon highballs, handed one to Clock.

"This I need," said Clock. "What a day. Woman's work nothing to what cops get—always something else coming along." He took a long grateful swallow.

"Anything interesting?" asked Jesse idly.

"Routine," said Clock. "Just routine. We've been busy most of the day on another damn fool suicide. Just making the hell of a lot more paperwork. No mystery, just more routine." He yawned and sampled his drink again.

After a little desultory conversation Nell swooped down on Davy and took him to settle him into bed, over the usual protests. "How's your offspring?" asked Jesse.

"Oh, flourishing." Fran smiled at him dreamily. "You know, Nell's right —it is a girl. It's got to be. Just right, with Davy being just over two years when she's born. And Esther or Judith—that'll be just fine."

"In the lap of the gods," said Jesse.

Clock yawned again and swallowed bourbon. "Suicides," he said. "It makes you wonder, you know. And I've seen a few. People with every reason to kill themselves—you'd think—terminal illness, whatever—they don't do it. And people who seem to be doing all right—no reason at all— they do it. It makes you wonder. But if there's one thing I've learned as a cop—who can understand human people?"

"Talking shop," said Fran. Nell came back and said she had got Davy off to sleep.

"People—they do come all sorts," said Jesse, thinking of Mrs. O'Reilly.

"Yeah," said Clock sleepily, "but it does make you wonder, you know. This one—an expensive condo, a lot of nice furniture, he was doing all right. The cleaning woman found him, this morning. He worked for a brokerage firm—looked as if he was in the money—all we've heard so far. Just a lot of paperwork to do. But it does make you wonder about people, not that you can come to any conclusion."

"Human nature," said Jesse.

"Funny name too," said Clock. "Don't know that I've ever heard it before. Kinsolving—Robert Kinsolving."

Jesse set his glass down with a little thump. "Kinsolving?" he said incredulously. "Robert Kinsolving? An address up on Electra Way? For God's sake! Suicide? That doesn't— Well, I couldn't very well believe— suicide? Are you sure it was suicide, Andrew?"

CHAPTER TWO

Clock looked at him curiously. "Don't tell me you knew him."

"I drew up a will for him last week, he was supposed to come in to sign it today. When he didn't show, the girls tried to track him down."

"That's funny," said Clock.

"Funny isn't the word," said Jesse. "Of all the candidates for suicide I'd say he was the unlikeliest. Damn it, I liked the man—a good man, a commonsensible man."

"Well, funny or not, there it is," said Clock. "What do you mean, am I sure it's suicide? It looks very typical. He shot himself, probably last night. We won't get an autopsy report for a couple of days, or a lab report."

Jesse rattled the ice cubes in his glass. "Damn it, I don't like it, Andrew. He wasn't the suicidal type, I'd swear."

"Is there one?" asked Clock.

"But," said Jesse, "oh, hell, I only met the man once, but you size people up. I'd have said the last man— And there's that will, for God's sake. If he'd decided to kill himself, for whatever reason, he'd have damn well signed that will first. He was a businessman, Andrew, and a pretty damned shrewd one. He wanted the sister to get everything. He'd know that if that will wasn't signed the estate would get split up. He said there are cousins."

"I've seen enough suicides to know that a lot of them do it on the moment's impulse. They're in a fit of depression, the gun or the sleeping pills are handy, bang, they do it."

Jesse said slowly, "He didn't strike me as an impulsive man, Andrew. I'd say above everything else he was the sound, steady businessman, not given to moods. Well, judge for yourself," and he told Clock about his one and only encounter with Kinsolving, all Kinsolving had said. Clock listened interestedly. The girls had drifted out to the kitchen to see about dinner. Clock held out his glass mutely and Jesse got them both refills.

"Well, I'm bound to say that might put a little different face on it, Jesse, but it still looks like the typical straight suicide. The cleaning woman found him—she comes Mondays and Thursdays, has a key to the place. He was on the couch in the living room, and the gun was under his hand. We'll be hearing from the lab, whether he fired it, about prints, but that's what it looks like. No evidence of any struggle or break-in, the place was neat and clean. Not even a used glass—the dishwasher had just a few dirty dishes in it. Sometimes the suicides get triggered off if they're halfway drunk—"

"Damn it," said Jesse, "that's woolgathering. He wasn't a drinker."

"How do you know?" asked Clock.

"Well, for God's sake, I don't know," said Jesse, "but I don't think I'm that stupid about sizing people up. Damn it, the man was a smart businessman, whatever else. He was a tax specialist, the fellow smart enough to hide money away from Uncle Sam, and my God, Andrew—Harlow and Wolfe—you can't get any more solid and conservative than that, and he'd been with them nearly twenty years. If he'd been given to drunken binges, he wouldn't still be with them."

"Well, I don't know," said Clock, "I don't say he was, but he might have been feeling depressed, just for once tied one on, and on impulse— The autopsy report will tell us about that."

"I don't like it," said Jesse uneasily. "Damn it, he'd have signed that will." He thought about Kinsolving, all Kinsolving had said to him. "He didn't strike me as a moody man—lonely, yes, maybe, a quiet fellow, he's had maybe a dull sort of life, but it suited him. He had interests, friends, he wasn't an unhappy man— Well, he did say he got a little depressed sometimes, but it didn't sound serious."

"Yes," said Clock, "but we don't know. That girl he was going to marry getting killed like that—maybe he brooded over it, even this long after."

Jesse stared at the remains of his drink. "All I say is, after a fashion I'm a hardheaded businessman too, and all my instinct says he'd have signed that will before he did it. You can say typical, you're the expert on suicides, but I don't like the feel of it, for God's sake."

"You can't be thinking he was murdered?" said Clock. "No evidence of any struggle or a break-in, and he doesn't sound like the kind of man to have any enemies, if you want to be melodramatic."

"I wouldn't have said so," said Jesse. "I just don't like the feel of it— I'll be interested in those reports. And damn it, this is going to make some work for me. What a mess. With that will not signed, I'll have to track down all the blood relatives, get the estate distributed, get the bank to administer it meanwhile."

Clock massaged his jaw. "Well, I'll take a closer look at the evidence after what you've told me, but I don't think there's anything in it. It looks pretty straightforward. I sent Pete to break the news to the sister—the cleaning woman gave us her name."

Nell looked in and said, "I've called you twice—everything's on the table."

They got up and Jesse said, "I'll have to see her too. I could bear to sit in on some of your investigation, Andrew."

"Be our guest," said Clock amiably. "The cleaning woman's coming in to make a statement in the morning, and I'll have to talk to the people at his office, just for form's sake. I see what you mean about the will, Jesse, but I've seen a hell of a lot of suicides and at least half of them do it on the moment's impulse. Probably," he laughed shortly, "regret it when it's too late."

"There wasn't any note—you'd have mentioned it. 'Goodbye forever, nobody loves me.'"

"Well, no, but that's not too unusual with a man. People," said Clock, "are funny. I never knew a female suicide who didn't leave a note, but the men don't always bother."

"For heaven's sake come and sit down," said Fran. "Why so serious, Jesse?"

Clock said, "He's thinking I'm a stupid cop."

"Just think you ought to look twice at this thing," said Jesse. "We'll put it up to you girls, neither of you stupid either, and I think you'll agree with me."

They listened interestedly, and did. Athelstane came to sit on Jesse's feet and beg for handouts, and Fran said disapprovingly that they ought to train him better, he was overweight now.

For once, Jesse hadn't any appointment on Tuesday, and after calling the Gordons, he drove directly down to Hollywood Division, the big rectangular building on Fountain Avenue, and found Clock sitting at his desk in the communal detective office talking to Detective Petrovsky.

"Andrew's been telling me what you said about Kinsolving," said Petrovsky interestedly. His round, snub-nosed face wore its usual amiable expression. "Puts a little different look on it, but not much. Funny about that will, but in the fit of depression he could have forgotten all about it."

"Thinking it over," said Jesse, pulling up a chair, "it strikes me as queer that he had a gun to hand. What kind was it?"

"A very damn funny little gun," said Clock. "A vest-pocket peashooter, a Spanish-made automatic, a thing called an Astra. I'd never run across one before, the lab identified it. They've still got it, of course. No, it's not registered to him, but that says nothing. The cleaning woman says she hadn't any idea he had a gun, she doesn't go prying into drawers."

The cleaning woman had a good deal more to say when she turned up ten minutes later, and none of it was very useful. Her name was May Bertrand and she was a widow in her fifties, big and rawboned and forthright. "I never had such a shock in my life," and surprisingly she accepted a cigarette and a light from Clock. "Mr. Kinsolving! He was such a nice man, always so polite, a real good man. A shame he wasn't married with a nice family, and such a nice-looking man too. And never an awful lot to do there, he was a real neat man, picked up after himself and never left a mess. Some men— And some women can be worse, at that. Those Cunninghams down the hall—I do cleaning for five of the people in that building, see—talk about messes! She's some kind of businesswoman, he's in electronics, and she can't even be bothered to stack dishes in the dishwasher, just leaves everything—clothes scattered all over, leaves the laundry for me to do—and Mr. Brenner, he's a widower, he leaves the mess around too. But Mr. Kinsolving, it was really a waste to pay me for two days' work, there was never much to do but the kitchen and bathroom floors and the vacuuming, he kept everything real neat and clean. He didn't have people in often, of course. And of course I hadn't seen much of him for the last year or so. I was there on Mondays and Thursdays, and of course he'd be off at work. A stockbroker he was, I suppose you know that. When he first moved in, that was about five years ago, I'd worked for the people lived there before, the Coopers—he died and she went to live with her daughter. And Mr. Kinsolving said he'd be glad if I came to him too. I was coming Thursdays and Saturdays then, so I'd see him sometimes on Saturdays when I was there. The only reason I could tell you about his sister, they were there one Saturday, I'd been late and they came, her and her husband, because he was taking them out to dinner, it was her birthday, and he introduced me."

"Do you know if he was much of a drinker?" asked Petrovsky. "Used glasses left around?"

She was indignant. "No, sir, never. Sometimes he had a friend come to see him, they played chess together, and there'd be the chess pieces left out and maybe a couple of glasses as if they'd had a friendly drink together, but he certainly wasn't a man to go getting drunk. He was a quiet one, never much to say for himself. Well, I'll tell you one thing to show you. It must have been about four years ago when I was still coming on Saturdays—I quit that when the Sherrells moved away and I decided to have my weekends free—I was there one day and he was home. Usually he'd be sitting reading, he wasn't much of a one for television, but that day he acted awful restless, he was walking back and forth, and after a while I asked him if anything was the matter, and he said he had a terrible toothache, he'd about decided to try and get an emergency appointment with the dentist. But just imagine, never saying a word about it till I asked. He was such a nice man, I never had such a shock in my life when I walked in there yesterday and found him." Her big frame quivered in remembered horror. "Right there on the couch, just lying back as if he was asleep, and it wasn't until I went closer I saw the blood—right over his eye—and then I saw the gun beside his hand. Oh! I nearly fainted away—I never knew he had a gun, well, how could I— And then I realized he'd shot himself, such a nice man, I always thought— It was just horrible, but I kept my head and called the police right away—"

Petrovsky had been taking notes, and typed the gist of that into a statement. She signed it in a painful scrawl. "You'll be asked to give evidence at the inquest," Clock told her. "We'll let you know when and where, probably later this week." When she had gone out, he shrugged at Jesse. "A handful of nothing."

"The sister and her husband are nice people," said Petrovsky. "All broken up. Couldn't believe it. Kept saying he was the last man to commit suicide."

"And I'd have said the same thing," said Jesse. "And she knew him. I want to talk to her, and I'll have to look at that apartment and open that safe."

"The lab's finished there now," said Clock. "A lot of work for nothing. We do have to go through the motions. They'll probably have picked up a few of Bertrand's prints, they got hers for comparison yesterday, the sister's and her husband's if they were there often, some of his friends. They'll have to sort them out to isolate any others, but there'll be nothing in it. Oh, there's this, but I can't see that it says anything either." He opened the top drawer of his desk and handed over something that looked like a button. "It could have been there for some time, I don't suppose the Bertrand woman moves the coffee table every time she runs the vacuum." Jesse looked at it curiously.

"What the hell is it?"

"Your guess as good as mine. One of the lab men found it when he was looking for the ejected shell casing. It was just under the front of the couch."

It was a small round pin about an inch in diameter, made of dull brass or jeweler's metal. Most of its front surface bore an ornate *B* in script; looking closer, Jesse could just make out two numerals below that, a *3* and a *5*. It was an anonymous little thing of small value. "It could have been there a while," said Clock again uninterestedly.

Jesse said absently, "He was shot over one eye? Isn't that fairly unusual?"

"You can't even say that," said Clock. "If they're using a gun, they go for the temple in most cases, but not always. They don't often try for the heart, the average person isn't that sure exactly where it is, and anybody knows a head wound is usually fatal. You're dragging your heels on this, but it can't be anything but suicide. There's not much more work for us to do on it. I'll have to talk to people at his office. If you want to take a look at the apartment, I've got the keys."

They drove up there in Clock's car. It was a newish, handsome condominium complex on a quiet street in upper Hollywood. Kinsolving's apartment was on the third floor. Clock unlocked the door, and they went into a square living room attractively furnished with a couple of comfortable leather-upholstered armchairs, a long brown leather-upholstered couch, mahogany end tables and coffee table. The carpet was a rich subdued tan, the drapes matching it. There was a little balcony off the opposite wall. If there was any stain of blood left on the couch, it wasn't visible. There was a big expensive stereo in one corner, its top propped open. Jesse went to look at it. There was a record on the turntable; whether just before he died or at some other time recently, Kinsolving had been listening to *Eine kleine Nachtmusik.*

"Neat housekeeper all right," said Clock. Except for the little disorder the lab men had left, dusting for prints, the whole place was very neat and clean. The kitchen counters were spotless and empty; there were only a few dishes in the dishwasher, the few he might have used for dinner on Sunday night. The bedroom was just as immaculate, a double bed neatly made up with a masculine-looking brown quilted spread, a tall mahogany armoire, a mahogany chest of drawers. Jesse opened the closet door and found the safe, standing under the rack of suits, slacks, and sports jackets. He grunted, switched on the overhead light, and got out the noted combination. When he got it open, he sorted through the contents and said, "Expectable." There were just the records of Kinsolving's financial assets: the statements of dividends from the money market funds, the fiduciary trust, income tax records for the last five years, a life-insurance policy, automobile-insurance policy, the pink slip on his car, a Buick sedan. The beneficiary of the life-insurance policy, not a large sum, was Mrs. Shirley Grant. "His car's here, I suppose," said Jesse.

"In the carport downstairs. We're finished here, you'll want his keys." Clock handed them over.

There was a small kneehole desk at one side of the living room; Clock rummaged through it and came up with a ledger from the top drawer. "Household and personal accounts. I'll have a look at it, but there's probably nothing relevant." The other drawers were largely empty; evidently he hadn't had or kept any correspondence except on business, and that would be at his office.

The small second bedroom was furnished as a den, with a modest-sized color TV, one comfortable armchair, one wall of tall bookcases. Jesse went to survey those with interest. There was one section predictably to do with Kinsolving's work, the classic works on government and economic systems, not a great deal of fiction, and most of that classic too: Dickens, Melville, Conrad, Kipling, very few modern writers. Most of the rest was nonfiction, showing a catholicity of taste: books on mountain climbing, archeology, anthropology, history, language. Surprisingly there was a little collection of poetry: again the classics—the *Oxford Book of English Verse*, *Scottish Ballads and Rhymes*, Shelley, Keats, Tennyson, A. E. Housman.

The place was fairly anonymous—the good furniture, the wardrobe of good clothes well maintained, the neat rooms—but Jesse felt it might contain a thin ghost, for a little while yet—the faint thin ghost of Robert Kinsolving, the quiet good man, the shrewd sensible businessman who had enjoyed his work, liked music and reading and chess, the occasional game of golf. The golf bag was in the hall closet, and the chessboard was set out with its pieces on a small table in one corner of the living room, with a pair of comfortable padded chairs facing each other across it. And that was all there was to see in the apartment; whatever ghost there might be was invisible.

The house on Oporto Drive was a sprawling old California bungalow with twin strips of lawn in front, some rose bushes beside the wide front porch. The long living room was pleasantly furnished with miscellany; in one corner was a very handsome and probably valuable old rolltop walnut desk. The Grants were both at home; of course, Alan Grant was a teacher and the school term was ended. He was a tall thin man with thinning dark hair, a rather craggy face with bushy eyebrows. Shirley Grant was small, just slightly overplump, with a round pretty face and curly brown hair.

They sat side by side on the couch and looked at Jesse and Clock; they were both obviously still shocked and shaken.

"I can't believe it," she said. "I still can't believe it, Bob was the last man in the world to commit suicide. The last man. You saying a fit of depression, but he didn't get depressed like that, ever. He was always just the same—he didn't have moods. It just isn't possible he's gone—" She put a hand to her head. "I told the realtor not to bring people to show the house—for a while. I just couldn't have people tramping through and having to be polite—with Bob—"

"He was a quiet fellow," said Grant, "but that's right, he wasn't one to get depressed or moody. I can't understand it—neither of us can."

"It must have been an accident," she said distractedly. "He'd never have meant to kill himself."

"Did you know he had a gun?" asked Clock.

"No, and that's why I say it must have been an accident. He wouldn't have known much about guns, he might have been just looking at it or something and it went off accidentally. We thought, yesterday after the other officer came to tell us, that he might have got it when he was living in the other apartment. Before he bought the condominium, he was living in an apartment on Los Feliz, and there'd been a little rash of burglaries there—he could have got it for protection then, but he'd never mentioned it." She uttered a dry sob. "Oh, I'm just thankful the children are at summer camp—they needn't know about it until they come home— they're so fond of Bob, and he was so good to them—" Grant had his arm around her shoulders.

"When did you see him last?" asked Clock.

"It was last Monday—a week ago yesterday—he came to dinner. He was just his usual self—the same as always—"

"Do you know if he had any women friends?"

She looked surprised. "Why, no—I don't think he'd been out with a girl since Marion was killed. Oh, that was such a terrible thing—they were so much in love, Marion was such a lovely girl—and the wedding all arranged, only two days off—she was buried in her wedding dress," and she sobbed a little again. "We hoped Bob would find another nice girl, get married, and have his own family, but he never did—he just couldn't forget Marion."

"Had he been well lately?"

"Why, of course, Bob was always well—" And catching the implication, she sat up straighter and said, "Do you mean you think he might have had something terribly serious, or thought he did, and that was why— Oh no, that couldn't be so. Bob was never sick, and he was a sensible man—if he'd thought there was something wrong, he'd have gone to the doctor to find out for sure. He didn't like doctors much, he never went unless he had to—"

"Did he have a regular doctor, Mrs. Grant?"

"He'd have gone to Dr. Hatfield, Dr. George Hatfield, he's our family doctor. But he never did unless it was necessary, like the time he had to go to Mexico for the company and had to be vaccinated. But he was never ill— It was funny in a way, when he had to go up before the draft board— that was years ago during the Vietnam war—they said he had a heart murmur and exempted him. But Dr. Hatfield said it wasn't anything to worry about." She sobbed again and her husband patted her shoulder. "The only time I ever remember Bob being seriously ill—we thought he might die, it was terrible, we were all scared to death— It was just after his twenty-first birthday—he was going to UCLA then—he had a strep throat and he was allergic to the antibiotic the doctor gave him, he had a terrible reaction and finally the doctor had to rush him into emergency—but in a day or so he was just fine. It just isn't possible he's gone—"

"It had to be an accident," said Grant positively. "And we've got to ask you—about when we can have him—arrange a funeral."

"The coroner's office won't release the body until after the inquest, Mr. Grant. You'll both have to appear, you'll be notified. You understand there has to be an autopsy." They nodded quietly.

"What about his apartment?" she asked drearily. "I just don't feel as if I could face sorting everything out."

Grant looked at Jesse. "You were his lawyer? I don't recall his ever mentioning your name."

"Very briefly," said Jesse. "There'll be details to sort out all right, and I'll want to see you again, I won't bother you with all that now. There's no particular hurry about settling matters—the estate will go on maintaining the apartment in the meantime."

"You'll be notified about the inquest," said Clock. "Probably sometime this week." They just nodded again.

Back in the car Clock lit a cigarette and switched on the ignition, automatically reaching to turn on the air-conditioning. "And that could be the explanation, even if it is pretty damned farfetched. Accident. I don't know how anybody could shoot himself in the head by accident, but it just could be. He wasn't a man to have known much about guns."

"I wouldn't think so," agreed Jesse.

"Obviously not, if he bought that damned useless toy for protection.

It's probably not accurate beyond a three-foot range. But automatics—
See what the lab boys say—they can sometimes be damned hair trigger, go
off if you look at them. It's just remotely possible that he'd got the thing
out to look at it for some reason and it was an accident. The lab and
autopsy reports should give us a better idea. Do you still want to tag along
with me?"

Jesse said irritably, "I've got an appointment at four o'clock. Everything
else can wait."

That old and solid firm of Harlow and Wolfe occupied a large office
complex on the fourth floor of one of the new highrise buildings on
Flower Street downtown. Everybody they talked to was shocked and
grieved to hear about Kinsolving; evidently he had been well-liked and
respected. Everybody was astonished to hear it labeled a possible suicide.
Wolfe, the only partner in, said heavily, "I'd have said the last man, but
who can tell what another man's feeling?"

The redheaded receptionist said, "Mr. Kinsolving—but he was always
so cheerful and friendly!"

The secretary in the office Kinsolving had shared said blankly, "I can't
believe he'd do such a thing, he just didn't seem that kind of man—why,
the very last time I saw him he was just fine, just the same as always. It
doesn't seem possible."

Nobody in the office had seen Kinsolving since last Thursday. "But
there wasn't anything unusual in that," said Harlan Jacobson. He had
shared this office with Kinsolving, a small office apart from the large outer
area, down one corridor where several individual offices were partitioned
off. Jacobson was a big heavy-shouldered man in his forties, with a nearly
bald head and cynical dark eyes. Right now he was looking shaken and
sorrowful. He sat back in his desk chair, the desk a clutter of papers held
down by his name sign, and got out a thin black cigar. "Like me, Bob was
in and out—he'd be calling on clients at their own places quite a lot.
Makes for goodwill, you know. He and I were the tax experts here, and
every now and then we'd be doing some traveling, looking into investment
possibilities. My God, I'd have said I knew Bob pretty damn well, this
really rocks me. As nice a fellow as you'd want to meet. Bob, killing
himself. It just doesn't make sense." He shook his head. The secretary
came back with a letter. "Oh, just leave that, Betty, I'll sign it after a
while."

Clock lifted a hand at her. "You did work for Mr. Kinsolving too?"

"Yes, that's right. I just can't get over this, he was just the same as always on Thursday." She was a thin dark girl about thirty, with slightly protruding teeth.

"You're Miss—"

"Mrs.," she said. "Mrs. Brett."

Clock reached into his pocket and showed her the little pin. "Would you recognize this? It seems to have your initial on it."

"No, I never saw it before."

"Were you ever in Mr. Kinsolving's apartment?"

"Certainly not," she said coldly. "Once in a while either he or Mr. Jacobson might ask me to do some overtime, if it was something urgent, but not often, and right here at the office." She went out looking curious and annoyed at the same time.

"Don't tell me," said Jacobson, "you're imagining that Bob had something going with Betty? The original ice maiden, if you want a personal opinion."

"Well, all right," said Clock, "as long as we're on the subject, would you know if he had any women friends?"

Jacobson shrugged. "I would not. I just don't know. Bob was a good friend of mine, and we talked about this and that, but he was close as an oyster about his personal affairs. He could have, but he never said anything to me about that."

"Would you know if he'd been worried about anything recently? Any of his business dealings, personal finances?"

"There wouldn't be anything like that," said Jacobson definitely. "Bob was a very sound man, and a damn cautious man when it came to advising clients or investing his own money. He had a nose for money, you could say. He'd made some damned good investments personally, and he'd made a lot of money for a lot of the people he was advising. I never knew him to go wrong. He wouldn't have had any financial worries, if you're thinking maybe that's why he did it. I'm damned if I can figure out why he did do it. He wasn't given to ups and downs, you know—he was the most even-tempered man I ever knew. My God, even that day when Upgrove came in here cussing him out and threatening to get him fired, he never turned a hair. Of course, he hadn't any real reason to, but all the same, Upgrove's a big bruiser and the language he was using—"

"Upgrove," said Jesse. "What was that about?"

Jacobson laughed shortly. "Well, that was another thing that shows what I just said—Bob had a nose, an instinct, about money. It was that Amalgamated Gold Medal Properties thing. Big outfit putting up condos,

apartment complexes all over, back in the Midwest and up north. Bob
went back to Tulsa to have a look at the first one that got finished, and it
looked like a very safe and sound deal. And profitable. Good return on
investment, but it was long-term. It was one of those deals where you had
to leave the investment in for a stipulated period, there was a penalty if
you wanted to take it out earlier. Bob had got four or five of his people to
go for it—this was last year—and then, let's see, it was around last January
that he got to feeling uneasy about it. Just on instinct. He couldn't exactly
put a finger on anything, but he just smelled something a little fishy, and
he got all but one of his investors to pull out, pay the penalty, and get
most of their money back. All but this Upgrove—he's co-owner of a
market chain and he sure as hell isn't hurting for money, but the more he
has, the more he wants, and who's to blame him? He wouldn't listen to
Bob, said the thing was good as gold and he wasn't going to let himself in
for the penalty. He wouldn't pull out the investment. Well, as usual, Bob
was all too right," and Jacobson laughed mirthlessly. "The balloon went
up at the end of May, I don't know if either of you noticed the newspaper
stories. Did it go up with a vengeance, gents!" He blew out a long stream
of cigar smoke. "I just thank God I hadn't got any of my people into it.
The general manager of the corporation—a fellow named Podmore—had
been getting into the accounts for a couple of years, and when a book-
keeper or somebody finally suspected something was wrong, Podmore out-
guessed the cops and took off with something like six million in cash and
negotiable bonds. They're still looking for him, the Tulsa cops, that is—
that's where their headquarters were. The company went into bankruptcy
and anybody who had any money in it lost every dime."

"Including Upgrove," said Clock.

"Oh, my God, he was wild," said Jacobson reminiscently. "He rushed
in here like a lunatic, raving mad and cussing at Bob a mile a minute,
threatening to get him fired for handing out the wrong advice, for God's
sake. Of course he was furious about the money—he dropped about a
hundred and fifty thousand—but he only had himself to blame. Bob had
advised him to pull out."

"Did he calm down and admit it?" asked Jesse.

"Not that one," said Jacobson. "When he'd used up all the cusswords
he knew, he marched out, and next day he pulled out his whole account
with us and transferred it to Walters and Finch in the next block. If he'd
listened to Bob—but listen, I can't tell you one thing about this, about
Bob's killing himself. I can't get over it, he wouldn't have had any reason."

"Well," said Jesse abruptly, "I'll be supervising the administration of the estate. Do you know if Kinsolving kept any personal records or belongings here?"

Jacobson shook his head. "I don't think so—just records of his clients' transactions. I tell you one fellow this is really going to shake up. Sam Ulrich. I guess he was about Bob's closest friend—they used to play chess together a lot. Ulrich was one of Bob's clients, he'd been with him a long time. A very nice guy, he dropped in here once in a while and they'd go out to lunch together. He inherited a chain of restaurants—doesn't do much work but oversee the management—follows the races and takes a trip to Vegas occasionally. Oh, I think he lives in Bel Air."

Clock looked through Kinsolving's desk, but there were only business records belonging to his clients and nothing Jesse would need. They came out of the building to the blinding glare of the hot July sun on the cement streets and started back to the parking lot.

"I hope," said Clock, "you're not thinking that Upgrove nursed a grudge for a couple of months and decided to murder Kinsolving."

"It doesn't seem very likely," said Jesse sadly. "It's just—like Kinsolving —I've got a sort of instinct. Damn it, Andrew, the idea of an accident is a very damned remote possibility, you just said so. And the momentary impulsive bit I don't buy either, because he doesn't seem to have been that kind of man. All I say is, whatever kind of reason he had or thought he had, he'd have signed that will first. I'd stake my current bank balance on it. He dealt with money—with assets—he was geared to thinking about money—he'd have waited another twelve hours to sign that will, damn it."

"It's a point," conceded Clock. "But even the smartest people do irrational things. He told you he knew he should have made a will long ago. Which he should have."

"And that's true too," said Jesse, climbing into the passenger seat. "And when I think of all the work it's going to make me—hell. Just because Mrs. Gorman happened to mention my name, he had to come to me."

"I suppose so," said Clock disinterestedly.

"Cousins, he said," and Jesse groaned. "God knows how many. I'll have to get a bank to hold the assets in the meantime. It'll have to wait until after the inquest. Find out from the sister just who all the blood relatives are, where they live. What with my fees and the bank's, if there are very many cousins, none of them is going to get much of an inheritance. And he wanted his sister to have it all. Damn it to hell, Andrew, he knew what dying intestate would mean."

"Don't say it again—he'd have signed the will. All I go by is evidence, and I know what this evidence looks like. The lab report will probably clinch it, and the autopsy report. They should both be in sometime tomorrow, and depending how busy the coroner's office is, they'll schedule the inquest for the end of this week or next Monday."

The cold rush of air-conditioning in the car was consoling. They didn't do much more discussing of it on the way back to Hollywood. "I could offer to take you out to lunch," said Jesse in the parking lot of Hollywood Division.

Clock looked at his watch and swore. "I may not get any—there are those witnesses to the latest heist due in to make statements. I'll let you know when those reports come in."

Jesse got out his keys and said, "By the way, had it occurred to you that that little pin could belong to the cleaning woman? Mrs. Bertrand."

"I was talking to her at the apartment when the lab man found it," said Clock. "She says she never saw it before, and she doesn't think it was there when she ran the vacuum last Thursday. But she admitted she hadn't pulled the coffee table out to vacuum in front of the couch. Well, I'll see you."

Jesse lifted a hand and started for the Mercedes.

At two o'clock that afternoon a very shaken and upset citizen arrived at Hollywood Division and demanded to see Clock. He was a short stocky sandy-haired man about forty-five, and he faced Clock with a belligerent jaw thrust out.

"Just what the hell is all this bullshit about Bob Kinsolving?" he demanded. "You saying Bob killed himself! That's the goddamnedest nonsense I ever heard! My God, I can't believe he's dead—Bob—shot? I can't take it in." He collapsed into the chair beside Clock's desk; he looked gray and sick, and Petrovsky brought him a paper cup of water, but he waved it away.

He was Sam Ulrich, and he said he'd been Kinsolving's closest friend. "We were going out to lunch together, and when I got to his office Jacobson told me— I never passed out in my life, but I damn well nearly did then. Bob, dead! Shot! And the police saying suicide. He never would have. I can tell you that, he never would have. My God, I was there last Saturday night—we got together for a couple of games of chess about twice a month—and he was just fine. He didn't have any worries, any trouble, and besides, I can tell you he'd never in this world have committed suicide! I know that for a fact." He accepted Clock's cigarette; his hand was shaking. "Listen to me. Bob and I'd been friends for years. A while back, three or four years, we got talking about suicide once—I don't remember how. And Bob said it was one conviction he had, that it was wrong. You see, he and his sister, they'd been brought up to go to church, Sunday school and all—the Presbyterian Church—but it hadn't taken with Bob, he wasn't very set on religion. But he said then—he was a great reader, you know, and he'd got sort of sold on this reincarnation thing—he said that was one principle he did believe, that it was wrong and foolish to kill yourself. That we're supposed to live out our natural lives and sort of cope with whatever troubles we've got. He'd never have killed himself."

"People say things and do the opposite," said Clock.

"Not Bob. My God, it doesn't seem possible he's dead—" But he calmed down after a while and answered a few questions. No, of course he wasn't the only friend Kinsolving had had—there were the Jacobsons, they'd had him to dinner once in a while and he'd take them out to restaurants—mutual friends he and his sister had known—an old school friend, Tod Bryson, and his wife— "He wasn't much of a socializer, but of course he had friends—"

"What about women friends?" asked Clock.

Ulrich stared dully at his cigarette. "I don't know. Maybe that sounds crazy, Sergeant, or as if I'm lying to you. But I don't know. You'd think—two men, good friends, that would have come up, he'd have said something—but I don't know. Bob was—a very private sort of guy. He kept his personal affairs to himself. It was a terrible tragedy, that girl he was engaged to—" Ulrich stabbed out the cigarette. "Once in a while, I kidded him—'Old-maid bachelor, why don't you find a nice girl to keep house for you'—and he'd kid me back—I'm a bachelor too. I don't know," said Ulrich. "But if there was some woman, it wouldn't have had anything to do with—what happened. Bob was a very levelheaded guy. He'd been crazy in love with that girl who got killed, I can't see him going overboard for another girl. But I can tell you straight, I knew him better than anybody else, and he'd never have killed himself intentionally."

"You'll probably be called for the inquest," said Clock. "You seem to have been the last one to see him, last Saturday night."

"All right," said Ulrich thickly. "But I can tell you—and anybody else —he'd never have killed himself. I'll never believe that."

CHAPTER THREE

Jesse was proofreading a contract at one-thirty on Wednesday afternoon when Clock called him. "Those reports are in, if you'd like to see them, it looks open and shut all right."

"All right, I'll come down," said Jesse. "Later—I've got an appointment in half an hour." The appointment was with Huff, who was all fired up to bring a countersuit on his wife, and it took a while to soothe him down and convince him he'd better stand pat. It was three-thirty when Jesse got down to the Hollywood Division and found Clock alone in the big communal detective office.

Clock told him first what Ulrich had said. "There's not much in that, of course. People don't always act logically, in fact, if I wanted to be cynical, I'd say damn seldom. It doesn't mean a damn that Kinsolving was acting normal on Saturday night, but for what it's worth, there it is."

"The reports," said Jesse.

"In a minute. I thought you'd like to see the gun. The lab just sent it back." Clock shoved the thing across the desk and Jesse picked it up gingerly. "It's not loaded. They used up the rest of the clip firing test slugs. It takes a load of six—.25 caliber." Clock looked at it disparagingly. "A damn peashooter."

It was a very small gun, hardly more than four inches long, square and black. "Oddly enough," said Clock, "it's not hairtrigger." He took it back and snapped the trigger to illustrate. The trigger went down with a deadly little click. "Doesn't take much pressure, but some. The damn thing looks like a kid's toy, but it's efficient enough at close range. The only thing I'd say, it doesn't seem to me it's a gun a man might buy for protection. But that doesn't mean anything either. I'm familiar with guns and Kinsolving wasn't. You can see the serial number's been obliterated, maybe filed off at some time, or just deteriorated with time. The damn thing's made in Spain, and the lab says there'd have been some dealers importing them from years back. It'd be a waste of time to try and trace it, no records to locate. You know how the law reads." Jesse said he did. "Kinsolving could have bought it anywhere at any time, a gun dealer's, a pawnshop. Most of them are honest, and he was an honest law-abiding man. The dealer would have told him about the waiting period and sent the routine inquiry to us to find out if he had a record. When we passed on the word he didn't, the dealer would just hand over the gun, explain that it would have to be registered if he wanted to carry it on him or in the car, but if he was just keeping it at home it didn't have to be."

"Yes," said Jesse. "It's a handy little gun."

"A damned peashooter," said Clock, scowling at it. "Going to buy a gun"—and absently he patted his left shoulder where the .357 Colt Python rested in the shoulder holster—"I wouldn't look twice at the damned thing, but as I say, I know about guns. Well, that's all there is to it. It's the gun that killed him—the slug in his head came out of it, a single slug, there were five left in the clip. I don't suppose the sister wants it, but you'll be listing it among his effects."

"I'll take it away sometime," and Jesse put it down on the desk. "What about those reports?"

Clock picked up the first of two manila envelopes on his desk. "Well, the autopsy report hasn't any surprises for us. He was a perfectly healthy specimen, no chronic troubles, and in excellent condition for his age. Bullet wound the sole cause of death. Estimated time, between 7 and 9 P.M. last Sunday night." Jesse held out his hand and Clock passed over the report. Skimming the technical jargon, he read it rapidly. There was a description of the wound in medical terminology, a technical impersonal description of the body: a well-nourished male, sixty-nine inches, a hundred and forty-five pounds, approximate age— "Um," said Jesse. "The blood-alcohol rate."

"Yes, well, Ulrich told us he wasn't much of a drinker," said Clock. "Usually had one highball before dinner, no more. Bourbon and water. There was just a half-full bottle of bourbon in the apartment. That's apparently what he'd had, just before a meal a couple of hours before he died, by the progress of digestion."

"Yes," said Jesse. "He'd have had the highball and then dinner, probably about six o'clock or a little later, and he was sitting in the living room listening to records. *Eine kleine Nachtmusik*—not the most cheerful thing he could have picked, but hardly gloomy enough to set him brooding over suicide. No, there's not much in it. What did the lab have to say?"

Clock said halfway reluctantly, passing a hand down his jaw, "Well, there's just one thing I'm wondering about, but I suppose there's nothing in it really." He took up the other report. "We saw how clean the place was, but practically anywhere you'd pick up all sorts of latent prints, partial prints, whether they're identifiable or not. There weren't many in that place. They got the Bertrand woman's to compare, and I sent Ulrich to be printed yesterday. They picked up some of Bertrand's in the kitchen and bathroom—that's natural—and Ulrich had left a couple on one of the chairs beside the chess table. Kinsolving's here and there everywhere else. And no others at all. The Grants hadn't been there in a while. He usually went to their place."

"All very natural," said Jesse. "What don't you like?"

Clock wasn't to be hurried. "His prints were on the gun, in the right places. Just at the right places, it was clean otherwise. And it's a damn small thing, but I'd have expected more. In my experience, if a man's contemplating shooting himself, he's going to be handling the gun—for at least a few minutes before he does it. I'd rather have expected a couple of prints on the barrel, the butt. But the size of that damned gun—" He shrugged. "It's six of one, half dozen of the other. There was an address book—I've got it here, if you want to look at it—but not many names in it, and only his prints. He wasn't a socializer. Probably most of the names in it were his clients, the people he was advising about investments. Apparently he had only a few close friends, by what we heard from Ulrich. I got hold of this other one, Tod Bryson, last night. He was at college with Kinsolving, they'd kept up—used to play golf together—but he hadn't seen Kinsolving for a couple of weeks, he'd been on a trip back East with his wife." Clock was looking over the lab report. "All right, here we are. They ran a neutron activation analysis, of course, to find out if Kinsolving had fired the gun. Tests for powder residue on his hand."

"I have heard of it," said Jesse mildly.

"Well, it was positive," said Clock, "but I'd have expected more residue. There it was, all right, but just a trace. But the size of that damned gun—and of course it wasn't anything like the charge in a heavier caliber, it's just a .25. I talked to the lab man who ran the test, and he said it was about what he'd expect from a gun that small."

"So that's that," said Jesse. "His hand was on the gun when it was fired."

"I said it was open and shut," said Clock. "I've got something else to show you." The ledger he had taken from Kinsolving's desk at the apartment was on the blotter before him; he picked it up. "This is fairly new— he'd just started making entries last November. I'd have a guess that when he used up a ledger, he'd stash it away somewhere. He was quite a one for keeping meticulous records. You'll probably come across some of the old ones on a closet shelf or somewhere. Well, of course, he was an accountant

—it'd be second nature to him." Clock opened the ledger. "I spent quite a while looking through this, and I spotted just one thing. Have a look and see if you notice it too."

Jesse took the big thick book and started to look through it. Kinsolving's neat copperplate hand covered only the first eighteen or twenty pages, the first date entered being November 21. He had kept the meticulous records all right, full and complete. There were the precise accounts of all his personal expenditures, the figures neatly delineated, the notations of everything he had spent, however minimal. It was the day-to-day record of the orderly life, the record of ordinary expenses; he had put down everything. The monthly maintenance fee on the condominium, purchases of groceries, payments to Mrs. Bertrand, cleaners' bills, gasoline bills, purchases of records, of books. A repair bill on the stereo. Dues at the Wilshire Country Club, a miscellany of running expenses. He had bought a couple of new golf clubs last February, a new suit in March, two new shirts, a pair of shoes just two weeks ago. Carefully recorded was the cost of haircuts every six weeks or so. He had bought a season ticket for the Hollywood Bowl in April; he had attended a performance of *Romeo and Juliet* at the Shubert Theater last month. The last notation, under the date of last Friday, was "Lunch at Hilton Gibson and self—$22.50."

"Gibson being one of his clients, I take it," said Jesse. "Yes, I think I see what you mean."

Clock took back the ledger. "He wrote everything down, even the damn haircuts, but here—and here"—running a finger down the pages—"we've got just a figure with no explanation. And the same figure every time, an even hundred bucks. That says to me—"

"I can have a guess too," said Jesse dryly. "The call-girl service."

"Maybe it's damn funny he'd enter it," said Clock, "but it was second nature to him to keep the careful records. He had to put it in, but just for himself he didn't need to set down what it went for. Well, he was human and only forty-one. And you can see it was apparently on a pretty regular basis, about once or twice a month."

"And very moderate," said Jesse amusedly. "Yes, that's probably it."

"And there'll be no way of tracing it down, which call girls they were, where. He was a man living on a set routine, and he'd very likely been patronizing the same service for a long time. I'd have a bet if you take a look at his older ledgers, the same figures will show up. He wouldn't have the phone number written down, he'd know it. There weren't many female names in the address book, and your Mrs. Gorman is one of them—

probably all clients. We can try to check, but I doubt if we'd come up with anything, and what the hell does it matter anyway?"

"Not much," said Jesse. "You're thinking that that funny little pin might have been lost by one of the call girls? It doesn't look like the kind of thing a flashy call girl would be wearing to meet a client."

"Oh hell, what does it matter?" said Clock roughly. "There'd have been other people in that apartment occasionally. There'll be an engineer for the building, checking up on the heating and air-conditioning, fixing the plumbing when it goes wrong. You notice he'd just had an upholsterer come to give him an estimate on reupholstering the couch. He didn't know anybody else in the building, we asked, but people don't neighbor in those places. But for all we know, Mrs. Bertrand may be friends with other cleaning women working there."

"No, there's not much in it," agreed Jesse.

"And just as we expected, the lab report clinches it," said Clock.

"Don't say I told you so," said Jesse plaintively. "But I'd like, for God's sake, to know why. Why in hell's name, Andrew? Here's a man doing damn well in life, a steady man, a sensible man, a respected businessman, maybe a lonely man, but he was a quiet one, didn't like to socialize much. He had a sister he was fond of, he had a few good friends. He got some quiet enjoyment out of life, with his golf and his music and his books, and the chess games with Ulrich. He liked his job and was good at it. He lived by routine, he was settled into bachelorhood and the humdrum daily round. He'd never shown any tendency to serious depression. He never got drunk, he didn't have any financial worries—for a man his age he was doing right well moneywise. There wasn't anything wrong with him physically. Why in hell's name should he suddenly commit suicide? Sitting there listening to the stereo on a quiet Sunday night, all of a sudden go and get that gun, wherever he kept it, and shoot himself? And Ulrich says he thought suicide was wrong. Everybody said it doesn't make sense."

"When did the vagaries of human nature ever make sense?" asked Clock. "People do these things, there's no point wasting time guessing about it. Maybe he got to brooding about that girl he'd been going to marry. Sitting there listening to the music. Maybe he was feeling extra lonely that night, maybe he thought he'd find the girl on the other side, if he believed in that. Nobody'll ever know now, that's for sure. The fact is, he did it, and that's that."

"And the rest is silence," said Jesse. "But it still sticks in my mind, Andrew—that will. Yes, it was second nature to him to keep careful records, have everything neat and tidy and arranged. He'd made an appointment to sign that will, just two days before. Say he had the sudden impulse, decided all of a sudden to get out of the humdrum daily routine, I still say, given the kind of man he was, he'd have remembered that will and not done it then. It wasn't a natural thing for a man like that to do."

"Suicide's never natural," said Clock. "As I say, most of the suicides I've seen did it on pure impulse. And who ever knows what's in another man's mind? It gets triggered off between two seconds. By all we've heard about him, he wouldn't have killed himself in his normal state, but nobody who commits suicide is in a normal state."

"Granted," said Jesse. "But I'd like to know what in hell set him off, that steady sensible fellow."

"We never will," said Clock. He'd been turning that cheap little pin round and round on his desk, and now flicked it with one finger in Jesse's direction. "You can keep that as a souvenir, to remind you that people don't operate like well-oiled machines. You can never predict human nature, there's no logic to it, or very damn little. The inquest is scheduled for two o'clock on Friday afternoon, by the way. It's one of the deputy coroners, Steiner, and he's a fussy little man—now *he* is predictable, and does operate on logic—he'll probably take a good deal of testimony and drag it out. It'll be a little ordeal for the Grants, poor people, but it can't be helped. Just one of those things. You'll be summoned to attend, one of the people who saw him last."

"Yes, poor people in another sense," said Jesse, getting up. "She'd have come in for a very nice bundle if that will had been signed. I add it up to around half a million."

"That much?" Clock was surprised.

"Maybe a little more. The condo alone— And it's going to be a hell of a nuisance to settle. Track down all the relatives, sell off everything, and divide it up. All the paperwork—"

"Don't mention paperwork to me," said Clock sourly. "We've got two new heists to work and we're shorthanded, Mantella off on vacation. And I haven't got around to a report on the latest homicide—nothing to work, just another idiot of a teenager freaked out on the combination of dope and liquor. You'd think anybody'd know better, but I swear most of the kids just don't have good sense these days." He yawned and passed a hand over his jaw, at this end of the day showing dark stubble. "And Fran saying she wants at least two—but I tell you, Jesse, sometimes it scares me thinking about bringing up the kids. You can try your damnedest—that dead teenager's parents seemed like nice respectable people—but with all the trouble waiting around to happen, the dope and the liquor and the fast cars, you never know."

"All you can do is the best you can. Yes, Nell's fine. She says now she's decided on Sarah, so it'll probably be twin boys."

"God forbid," said Clock. "I'm in no hurry to go through that again, thanks. Fran saying maybe next year and now she'd like a boy. My God."

"Well, my father won't agree with you. As far as he's concerned, the more grandchildren the merrier."

"And he's going to spoil the baby rotten," said Clock grumpily.

"So I'll see you at the inquest." As Jesse went out, Petrovsky passed him towing a big black fellow, presumably a suspect in for questioning.

But that damned will stayed in his mind, the little riddle of Robert Kinsolving. He hashed it over again with Nell after dinner, distracting her from her book. "Damn it, why? Why the hell? The man hadn't had a brainstorm, a sudden fit of any sort, it'd have shown up at the autopsy. And I know everything Andrew says is so, it's mostly the momentary impulse, but damn it, Nell, I still have the gut feeling he'd have remembered that will. All his life was built around the handling of money—not that he seems to have been greedy for it, didn't make money a god—but it was his job, and he was damn good at it. I don't care what was in his mind, brooding over his lost love or what—and that was sixteen years ago, if he'd been that shattered over it he'd have killed himself then, not last Sunday night—I don't give a damn what was in his mind, he wouldn't have forgotten that will."

Nell watched him pace the floor. "You can't know that," she said sensibly. "Whatever was in his mind might have made him forget all about the will. Just as Andrew said, suicides aren't thinking rationally. At any rate, nobody'll ever know now."

"Damn it, I could wish he hadn't picked me, that's all," said Jesse gloomily. He realized that he might not be thinking rationally about Kinsolving, but Kinsolving had disturbed him in some depth of his being. For better or worse, he had a logical mind too, and the same kind of common sense as that quiet good man. The notion that some sudden quirk of the mind, some brain cell changing direction for a second or two, could rob any man of his good sense between one moment and the next, was profoundly worrying. There but for the grace of God—

"The mind of man is froward and strange," he muttered. "So Solomon

tells us." When that could happen to a man like Kinsolving— Unprecedentedly he went to get himself another drink.

"Don't fuss about it," Nell advised him patiently. "It's just another job at the office, darling."

"The way to look at it. I suppose you're right. But when I think how much trouble he's made by leaving that will unsigned, I'm feeling damned annoyed at the man. You're absolutely right. And I have a hunch that Andrew's right when he says probably the suicides regret it the minute it's done. Poor devils, not realizing what they're letting themselves in for—the consensus of all the communications that have come through—it's not a very good idea. Apparently they land in a pretty damned unpleasant place, for a while at least."

"I'd like to think," said Nell, "that he'll find his girl eventually. Speaking of which, what's William up to lately, anything interesting?"

"Not very," said Jesse. "Those cross correspondences—it's the same tiresome old stuff. Talk about human nature—my God. You'd think all the diligent psychic researchers would have proved it to everybody's satisfaction by now, survival and all the rest of it. But they will be so damned singleminded. Logic! They're all just too damned logical, which doesn't square with human nature."

"How do you mean exactly?" asked Nell, wrinkling her brow.

He sat back in the armchair, long legs outstretched, and swallowed bourbon. "Well, damn it, there'll always be the hardheaded skeptics who simply won't look at the evidence. They take the attitude that there can't be any evidence for impossibilities, so why bother to look? And you'll never get them to. But the parapsychologists are the hell of a lot stubborner, just because they're so damned logical. They just won't believe that the skeptics can't be reached if they produce enough watertight evidence—and so they go on doing it time after time, turning up all the same kind of evidence on all the different aspects of it, it gets monotonous. They keep trying to shove the skeptics' noses into it, and they'll never understand that the typical unbeliever will never be convinced."

"I see what you mean."

Jesse laughed sleepily. "The only way a skeptic's going to be convinced is to die, and feel very damned surprised to find out he's still there and the researchers were right all the time."

Nell yawned. "Well, I think I'll go up and finish my book in bed. And I can't help what the doctor says, I've gained another three pounds—that diet list be damned, I get hungry."

"Eating for two." Jesse followed her upstairs. She went to look in on

Davy, and he started to undress in the big master bedroom. Athelstane had padded up after them, and Murteza was already sound asleep in the middle of the bed.

But as he hung up his jacket, Jesse found himself hoping sentimentally that Kinsolving would catch up to his girl, somewhere, somehow. For whatever unfathomable reason, he had taken his own life, but he had known the folly of that intellectually, and sooner or later might find himself in a better place than he was probably in now. As it was, he had left unfinished work behind him for somebody else to do, and the immediate somebody was Jesse.

He had to be in court at another divorce hearing on Thursday morning, but it didn't take up much time; the judge was prompt and it was a straightforward affair. He got back to his office at eleven-thirty, and Jean said, "I set up an appointment for you with Mr. Howard at the Security Pacific Bank up the block. Two o'clock."

"Fine. I ought to be back by four. If I'm late, just apologize to Mr. Huff." He was getting tired of Huff and would be glad to get that business settled.

"And Mrs. Gorman called," said Jimmy, and laughed when he groaned. "She's had a spat with her niece and wants to leave the opal jewelry to somebody else."

"That woman," said Jesse indulgently.

"She's coming in on Monday morning. She wanted to see you tomorrow, but of course you're busy."

"Too true."

He took himself out to lunch at a nearby coffee shop and at two o'clock was closeted with Mr. John Howard of the trust department of a Security Pacific Bank. He handed over all Kinsolving's papers, and explained the position. "You can see it'll be a little chore to settle up. Have to locate all the relatives, get everything disposed of. We may have to sit on that condominium awhile, real estate is slow these days."

"Well, at least he didn't leave any outstanding debts," said Howard. "That's rather a queer little tale, Mr. Falkenstein. An enterprising, fairly young man like that. He'd got together a nice estate, hadn't he? Do you have any idea how many relatives?"

"Not a clue. I'll have to talk to the sister. Meanwhile, you can take charge of it. The monthly maintenance on the condo is due on the eighteenth of the month, he'd just paid it."

"Yes, we'll take care of that. I see"—Howard was looking through the bankbook—"he had a nice checking balance with us, the branch downtown. We'll keep it all together here, and I'll send you regular reports until we can sell out and get it distributed."

They went downstairs and set up the machinery on an account for Robert Kinsolving, Deceased. "What about the funeral?" asked Howard.

"I don't know what the Grants might arrange, I haven't talked to them. I don't suppose they have much loose cash, he's a teacher and there are two children. I'll be seeing her. I suppose there won't be any difficulty about getting the estate to pay for the funeral."

"Oh, no, no trouble about that, just a formality, and there's the little life insurance. You'll be in touch then. We'd better put the condominium on the market immediately, the sooner we can realize all the assets and get to the distribution the better. The complex manager will have a key."

Jesse agreed, and got back to the office just as Huff arrived, then spent a boring forty minutes listening to him castigating his mercernary wife.

The deputy coroner, Steiner, was the fussy little man Clock had described. The inquest was held in a basement room of the Central Criminal Court, next to the coroner's office. As usual, a rather motley jury had been assembled, four women and eight men. They were looking poker-faced and self-conscious.

Ulrich was called first, as the last person known to have seen Kinsolving, and he annoyed Steiner by expanding his answers and insisting that Kinsolving couldn't have killed himself.

"I'm sure we all sympathize with you in the loss of your friend," said Steiner, sounding remarkably unsympathetic, "but I must remind you that we are here not to listen to opinions, but the facts of the evidence."

"I tell you, I knew the man like a brother, and he'd never have done such a thing," said Ulrich loudly. "I think he was murdered."

"I cannot listen to irresponsible statements," said Steiner sternly. "Do you have any information to give us as to any person who might have had a motive for killing Mr. Kinsolving? You have just told us that he was a man respected in his profession and liked by everyone who knew him."

"Well, no, I can't imagine why anybody would have wanted to kill him —but I know he never did it himself," said Ulrich belligerently.

"That is your opinion and does not constitute evidence. Thank you. That's all we will ask you."

Shirley Grant was called next, very briefly. She was looking smart in a

tailored navy dress and a small hat with a half veil. She testified as to the
last time she had seen her brother, as to his good spirits at the time.
Steiner only asked her a few questions and dismissed her. But she hesi-
tated before stepping down, and then said in a clear strong voice, "I would
just like to say that I'll never believe my brother killed himself intentionally. I agree with Mr. Ulrich that he was—temperamentally incapable of
such a thing. I am convinced it must have been an accident."

Steiner looked at her over the top of his spectacles and said frigidly,
"Thank you very much, Mrs. Grant, that will be all."

Mrs. Bertrand gave voluble evidence of the finding of the body and
expanded on her terrible shock and the general niceness of Mr. Kinsolving. Steiner got rid of her in five minutes.

Jacobson was called and testified to Kinsolving's sound financial situation. Steiner didn't keep him long, and called Jesse. He elicited the bare
information about the unsigned will, which he obviously didn't consider
too important. "You had not met Mr. Kinsolving previously? This was the
first piece of legal work you had done for him? Exactly. So you can hardly
give us an opinion of his mental state."

"I had certainly set him down in my mind as a very sound man of
business. The most I can say is that there must have been some very
strong reason why he did not sign his will."

"But he could scarcely have done so, Mr. Falkenstein. He was dead.
Thank you, that is all."

He spent a good deal of time with Clock, asking about all the details of
the police evidence. Jesse's attention wandered to the body of the court;
there weren't half a dozen people present, just the witnesses the deputy
coroner had considered relevant. The Grants were sitting together in the
front row of chairs, and next to Shirley Grant was a tall thin old lady with
a grim expression.

Steiner had the lab report and autopsy report before him on the bench.
He led Clock patiently through the details of the laboratory examination.
"Then it is proven beyond doubt, by the scientific examination of the
body and the weapon, that Mr. Kinsolving was holding the weapon when
it was fired."

"Yes."

"I do not suppose that the jury are familiar with such a scientific test, it
may be helpful if you would elaborate on just what it consists of."

Clock, looking a little better tailored than usual in a dark suit, was
obviously bored. He looked at the jury. "It is called the neutron activation
analysis. The hands of the deceased are swabbed by chemically inert cot-

ton swabs. These are then moistened with a weak solution of nitric acid. The laboratory then tests the swabs for the presence of nitrate, that is, the residue left from gunpowder. If the deceased has fired a gun recently, the residue will be identified as present."

"That is very clear. And the laboratory found such residue on Mr. Kinsolving's right hand?"

"Yes."

"He was right-handed?"

"Yes."

"I trust the jury has followed this somewhat technical evidence. Mr. Kinsolving was then holding the gun when it was fired. Now, Sergeant, was there any evidence that anyone else had been present in the apartment at the time?"

"No. Not scientific evidence," said Clock neatly. "There was evidence that other people had been there from time to time, of course, but it's impossible to say how recently."

"But if another person had been present when the tragedy occurred, he or she must have notified the authorities at once?"

"I would certainly think so, but of course—"

"Very good. Thank you very much, Sergeant, I think that is all. I will just read certain excerpts from the autopsy report to the jury." Steiner cleared his throat and adjusted his glasses. "It is clearly indicated that Mr. Kinsolving was in excellent health, and we have heard that he seemed to have had no worries of any kind. As the autopsy report says—" The jury didn't look as if they enjoyed the details of the autopsy report, but they listened patiently. "People frequently commit suicide for very little motive or no motive at all. After the fact, it is impossible for us to judge what imagined motive there may have been for such an act. But you have heard all the evidence in this matter, and I shall now ask you to declare what type of death this was in law."

The jury didn't move out of the box, but by voice vote brought it in suicide. Steiner thanked them gravely and dismissed them.

Jesse went over to the Grants. She introduced him conventionally to the old lady, Mrs. Culver; that would be the aunt Kinsolving had mentioned. He said to Grant, "They'll release the body now and you can arrange for the funeral. The estate will pay all the costs."

"Thank you," they said in unison. They were looking tired and grave.

"And I won't trouble you now, but I'll have to talk with you about that. The estate."

"Oh yes," she said vaguely. "I suppose so."

"If you'll let me know about the funeral"—he gave Grant a card—"we can make it after that. I could come to the house."

"That would be all right," she said, sounding not much interested.

"Where do we go about the body?" asked Grant.

"Right here—the coroner's office down the hall." He watched them out. The jury had already gone, back to its workaday world, and Steiner was just disappearing through the door behind the bench. And so that was the end of Robert Kinsolving, thought Jesse. Or very nearly. The puzzle of Robert Kinsolving. And he hadn't any appointments for the rest of the afternoon; he'd go home early, and borrow one of Nell's library books or soothe himself with Bach.

Grant called him at home on Saturday evening. "The funeral's to be on Monday morning, at Forest Lawn. Ten o'clock."

Jesse thanked him for calling. "Would it be convenient for me to see you both that afternoon? I know it's a difficult time for you, but there's necessary business to get through."

"Yes, I understand that," said Grant. "That'll be all right."

"Say three o'clock? I'll see you then." And human nature was human nature; it was obvious that they'd been fond of Kinsolving, and grieved for him, but they undoubtedly suspected that she'd come in for what he had to leave, and he was going to be giving them another shock.

When he parked in front of the old bungalow on Oporto Drive on Monday afternoon, he noticed that there was a realtor's sign planted on the front lawn. Shirley Grant let him in; she was still wearing the dark dress she'd presumably worn to the funeral. In the long living room they sat side by side on the couch, and she told him dully, "The children will be back on Wednesday. I haven't told them—I just didn't know how to— and with everything in such a turmoil— The realtor doesn't think we can sell the house very soon, and Alan has to be up at the university on September third. There's Bob's apartment—"

"There isn't any particular hurry." He started to tell them about the will, spelled out the general situation, told them what he had done, what had to be done. "The estate will have to be distributed equally to all the blood heirs, and I'll need all the names and addresses you can give me. He mentioned that there were cousins."

"Oh, I see," she said numbly. "I didn't know about all that."

"If you ask me, it's very damned queer about that will," said Grant. "That wasn't like Bob."

"Yes, it's a pity, but there it is." Jesse got out his pen and notebook. "If you can give me the names—"

She put a hand to her head. "Heavens, I can't, Mr. Falkenstein. I don't know any of them, Bob and I have never met any of them. Dad had an older sister, she was about ten years older, and there'd been some disagreement between them—that was before either of us was born, I think—he never corresponded with her or talked much about her. She had a family, I don't know all the names—Aunt Janet just mentioned them casually."

"They're just strangers," said Grant, looking suddenly angry. "Bob wouldn't have wanted them to get any of his money—he didn't know them."

"Well, as he died intestate, that's how it has to be, Mr. Grant," said Jesse equably.

She put a hand on her husband's arm. "It doesn't matter, Alan," she said in a low voice, and her eyes held pain. "That's how it is. He just couldn't have known what he was doing. You'll have to ask Aunt Janet, Mr. Falkenstein. Mrs. Culver. She's kept up with some of them, she'll be able to give you some names and addresses. She was the youngest of the family, Dad's youngest sister. Mother was an only child and didn't have any relatives left at all when she died. Aunt Janet came back to California after her husband died—she never had any children. She has an apartment in Glendale. I could call her and ask if it would be all right for you to go and see her right now."

"Well, I'd appreciate it, Mrs. Grant. I'm very sorry about this, but that's just the way it is. It can cause a lot of trouble, legally speaking, when someone dies intestate like this."

She got up silently and went into the adjoining den. Grant was looking very angry now. He said, "It's a damn shame. Bob would have wanted Shirley to have everything. You said that's how he told you to make that will. And I expect he had quite a lot to leave. He was pretty smart about investing. Damn it, it's not that we're vultures, to think about the money more than Bob—but it doesn't seem right. These people, they'll just be second and third cousins, nobody he knew or cared about. I can't understand why he didn't sign that will. Oh, hell. Of course he was dead. And Shirley's right, it had to have been an accident. It had to be. It doesn't matter what that damfool coroner said or the jury. Bob enjoyed life, he wouldn't have wanted to die. It was an accident."

She came back and said, "She'll be glad to see you right away, Mr. Falkenstein. It's Mountain Street in Glendale." She had copied down the address for him.

"Thanks very much. This is all something of a mess, and I'm sorry it had to happen this way, but that's the way it is."

"It doesn't matter," she said, and she sounded very tired. "The money wouldn't make up for losing Bob."

"You'll get something, you know. When the estate is sold and distributed."

"And I'll bet Bob is turning in his grave," said Grant hardly.

When he found the address, it was a new starkly rectangular apartment building with sparse landscaping around the front. Mrs. Culver's apartment was on the top floor, down a thickly-carpeted hall. She opened the door to him promptly; she looked as grim and forbidding an old lady as he'd ever met, tall and thin with a high-bridged nose and piercing dark eyes, her gray hair in a severe knot on top of her head. Her thin face was innocent of any makeup and she was wearing a plain cotton housedress and uncompromising flat-heeled oxfords.

She looked him up and down and said, "Shirley told me about that will and why you wanted to see me. Come in and sit down. At least you look like a sensible man."

The living room was furnished with starkly modern pieces, almost a ludicrous contrast to her age and forbidding demeanor. "It's very funny about that will," she said. "Bob didn't know any of the cousins. He was a smart businessman. But Shirley is convinced it was an accident, and I believe it too. He wouldn't have killed himself, not intentionally."

"Well, can you tell me some names and addresses, Mrs. Culver?" He sat down on a fat gold tub chair.

"Yes, I can tell you some of them. Celia was the oldest of us, then Joe and then me. Celia was seven years older than Joe and I was six years younger than him. Celia married a man named Roswell, he was a minister, and they moved up north, to Eureka. Joe just detested that man, and I can't say I liked him any better. He was one of those sanctimonious ministers, always looking down his nose and quoting Scripture. Joe had a row with Celia after something he'd said about the man, and they never had much to do with each other after that." She was planted in the chair opposite him, feet firmly on the floor, speaking in a flat voice. "But I exchanged letters with her once in a while until she died—that was nearly ten years ago. I can tell you something about the family. Celia had a boy and a girl, Gregory and Ruth—they'll both be in their sixties now. Greg went into the ministry too—it's the Pentecostal Church—and he's married, had a boy and a girl too. I can't say I've kept up with them exactly. I've never laid eyes on any of them, and the second generation—but we exchange Christmas cards, that's about all. I can give you Greg's address —of course both Celia and her husband are gone—Greg lives in Eureka. There's a son and a daughter, they're both married with children. Ruth married a man named Harold Rayner, he's the manager of a big farm outside Yuba City. They've got children too, a couple of married daughters—I don't know the names, but I can give you the Rayners' address and they'll know." She got an address book from a small desk across the room and read out names and addresses.

"Thanks very much."

She opened her mouth, shut it, and then said suddenly, "And I wasn't going to say anything about it. The man's dead and gone, and it can't matter to anybody now, but I was brought up to tell the truth and shame the devil, and I reckon maybe his lawyer ought to know. At first, I thought —when Shirley called me—least said, soonest mended. But maybe his lawyer ought to know. Only I hope Shirley won't have to know—it'd be a terrible shock to her. Why, he didn't know himself."

"Know what, Mrs. Culver?"

She said baldly, "He wasn't their natural son, you see. They just raised him. And he was a good son to them, it all turned out just fine."

Jesse looked up from his notebook. "You mean he was adopted?"

"Oh, no," she said. "They never adopted him legally. They just took him and raised him."

Jesse dropped his pen and stared at her aghast. Mentally he felt that a yawning chasm had opened up before him.

"It can't matter to anybody now," she said. "The man's dead and gone, and it doesn't matter. I just thought maybe his lawyer ought to know."

CHAPTER FOUR

"Mrs. Culver, are you sure about that, that there was no legal adoption?"

"Why, yes, I know that. What's the matter? It isn't important now he's dead, is it?"

Jesse retrieved his pen and said, "I don't think you realize the implications of what you've told me, Mrs. Culver."

"What do you mean? Bob's dead and it can't matter to anybody, but I hope Shirley won't have to know, that's all."

"Yes, he's dead," said Jesse, "and he didn't leave a will. Now you tell me this, Mrs. Culver, don't you realize that if there was no legal adoption this changes the whole situation? None of these people are blood relatives, and they can't inherit any of his estate."

She looked at him in sudden consternation and confusion. "You mean Shirley won't get anything? But that's not right. It couldn't be right, Mr. Falkenstein. I don't care what the law says, Bob was Joe and Etta's son to all intents and purposes, even if he wasn't their natural son, and Shirley's own brother. I shouldn't have told you, but I thought—"

"Where did they get him?" asked Jesse. "Who were his parents, do you know?"

"Oh, for heaven's sake," she said, "I was the world's biggest fool to say anything about it! No, nobody knows, and what on earth does it matter now? He was a good son to them, a good brother to Shirley."

Jesse saw the chasm gaping wider and deeper. He shut his eyes briefly and said, "I'll spell it out for you, Mrs. Culver. If he wasn't legally adopted, none of these people have any claim on his estate. There'll have to be an attempt made to find out if he had any blood relatives, who his parents were. If there are any, if we can find them, they'll be due to inherit."

She looked at him incredulously. "Why, that's just crazy," she said. "After all this time? Joe and Etta had him since he was born! Nobody could find out who his real mother and father were now, that's just crazy."

"Well, that's how the law reads, I'm afraid. Where did they get him? What do you know about the circumstances?"

"Oh, I wish I'd cut my tongue out before I told you!" she said bitterly. "I never heard of such a thing, it's not right or fair, some girl who didn't care a button for him, just giving him away to strangers. It's just crazy. You mean that's the law?"

"That's the law," said Jesse. "Where did he come from, Mrs. Culver, do you know? Was it an adoption agency? But you said they didn't adopt him legally? Why not?"

"Oh, why did I have to open my mouth?" she said angrily. "I didn't know all that, it's just not fair. I expect he left quite a lot of money too—Bob was a smart man."

"Well, now you have told me, you'd better tell me whatever else you know about it. Where did he come from?"

She looked at him, her mouth pinched tightly and her eyes wet. "This is going to be an awful shock to Shirley. I should have kept my mouth shut —I never had any idea about what you said, about how the law says she wouldn't get any of his money. But nobody'd ever be able to find out about him after all this time."

"We'll have to try," said Jesse.

She sat up straighter and gave him a fierce look. "And suppose you can't —and you never will, nobody could—what happens to Bob's money then?"

"It would go into escheat."

"And what in the name of goodness does that mean?"

"It means the state would get it."

She looked even more incredulous. "You mean the government would get it all? That's the unfairest thing I ever heard, it's just not right!"

"You can look at it that way," said Jesse, "but that's the law. You can see that you'd better tell me anything you know about him."

She didn't say anything for a while, staring into space, and then she said slowly, "I just reckon you're right. Now it's out, I can't leave it there and not say anything else. I'm just downright sorry that Shirley's got to know about it. It'll be a terrible shock to her."

"How did they come to take him?" asked Jesse. "What do you know about it?"

She took a deep breath and let it out in a long sigh. "Well, the mischief's made," she said flatly, "and I see I've got to tell you. But I don't know much to tell you at that. I was back in Chicago at the time. You see, my husband Archie—I met him when he was out here visiting some cousins, and one of them was a friend of mine, that's how we met. And his father and uncle owned a big furniture store back there, he worked for them, and we went back there when we got married. Times were pretty bad for everybody in the Depression, and after the war, what with one thing and another, I never got back here for a visit until twenty years ago, and after that I never saw Joe and Etta again until I came back to live here after Archie died, and that was just a year before Joe died. But we always wrote pretty regular. All right, I'm getting to it, just give the old lady time. You see, Joe and Etta'd been married nearly fifteen years and never had any family. I don't know whether you know, Joe was a pharmacist and had his own store up on Sunset Boulevard. They'd started to buy the house when they got married. They had a pretty bad time through the Depression, but they managed to weather through. Etta used to help him in the store. It was a grief to them, not having any family, and Etta went to the doctors and all about it, but it wasn't any good. So they went to an adoption agency, a place run by the city. I don't know if you know about that, you're just a young man, and I think it's different now, but back then those places were awfully fussy about giving babies away for adoption. Etta said they asked about a thousand questions, how much money they had and how they lived and did they go to church, and a woman came and snooped all around the house. Wanted to know everything about them. And finally they put them on the waiting list for a baby." She drew another long breath. "I expect it's all different now with all the girls running around having illegitimate babies all the time, and those agencies just glad to hand them out to anybody, but back then it was different. Well, they waited and waited, and they didn't get a baby. And then they had a letter from the agency saying they'd been taken off the list of prospective parents because they were both over forty and the agency's policy was that they didn't let people that old adopt babies. Of all the fool notions. My mother was nearly forty when I was born—plenty of people have babies that late and seem to raise them all right. But that's what they said. Joe was mad as fire and Etta was too, but there wasn't anything they could do about it, you can see that. And then it was just like fate, the way it worked out, this baby turned up."

"Where?" asked Jesse. "How?"

"Well, it was queer—just like fate," repeated Mrs. Culver. "It was the neighbors. The people who lived next door, and I can't say the name, it's right on the tip of my tongue, I'll think of it in a minute. They owned the house next door. They were a good bit older than Joe and Etta, but they'd been neighborly—they used to play cards together with Joe and Etta. Their family was grown—I forget whether they had one or two if I ever knew. Anyway, it was some relative of theirs, a niece or something, who

knew about the baby. Whoever it was knew some girl who was going to
have a baby and wanted to give it up, and knew about Joe and Etta
wanting a baby."

Jesse sighed. "And you can't remember the name?"

"I will in just a minute."

"Where were they living then?"

"It was Serrano Avenue in Hollywood. They didn't get the house paid
off until way after the war, but they finally did. And then the funny way
things happen, about a year after they took the baby, Etta got pregnant.
You know it happens that way sometimes, people married for years and
after they adopt a baby they'll have one of their own. Bob was about
eighteen months old when Shirley was born. Crossley!" she said suddenly.
"Simon Crossley. I don't recall his wife's name if I ever knew it. I seem to
remember he had a printing business. They lived next door, and it was
some relative of theirs knew about the baby."

"All right," said Jesse. "Why didn't they adopt him legally? You're sure
they didn't?"

"Yes, I'm sure, because I had a little argument with them about it. I
thought they ought to, but they were afraid to try. On account of what
that agency had said. Etta was scared to death, if they applied to adopt
him, some state authority could say they were too old to have a baby and
take him away to give to somebody else. They just took him—he was only
a few days old when they took him, and I was the only one who knew
about it. Joe still wasn't having anything to do with Celia, and that holier-
than-thou husband of hers would have said this and that about bastards.
They just let Celia think the baby was theirs, and asked me not to tell her
about it." She was looking fierce again. "And he was theirs—some girl not
caring about him at all, just handing him over, and they gave him a good
raising and Bob was a good son to them."

"Did they know the mother's name?"

She shook her head. "If they did, they didn't mention it to me. I will
say they weren't so foolish as to just take him without checking up some.
Etta said the girl told them both the mother and father were white and
came of decent families. And as soon as they got him, they took him to be
checked by the doctor, and the doctor said he was a nice normal baby,
nothing wrong with him. And that's how it turned out. Bob was just fine,
and a smart boy, they never had any trouble or worry with him—he always
got high marks in school, and they were so proud of him. It's a wonder he
wasn't spoiled, the way Etta doted on him, but I guess Shirley coming
along kind of put an end to that." She sat back and sighed. "But you can

see, there'd be no way to find out who his real parents were after all this time. Forty-two years, heavens above. I just can't get over what you say about the money, that Shirley won't get any of it. The government getting it, it's the unfairest thing I ever heard—just because they didn't adopt him. I said they ought to have, just to have it all clear."

"He didn't know about it?"

"No, they never told him. Didn't see any reason to. As far as everybody was concerned, they were his parents," she said defiantly. "And Shirley was his sister. They were a family. And after all this time, to think it has to come out—and the government getting all the money—it's just not right. Oh, I wish to goodness I'd never told you, but I didn't know it'd cause all this trouble," she said wretchedly. "I suppose Shirley will have to know."

"I'm afraid so, Mrs. Culver. When it involves his estate."

She was silent and then said, "I certainly don't look forward to it, but I reckon I'd better be the one to tell her. It'll be an awful shock to her. And to think if I hadn't opened my mouth and told you, nobody'd be any the wiser, and she'd have got some of the money at least."

"Well, it's always better to get at the truth," said Jesse. But he reflected that on the whole it might have been just as well if she had kept her mouth shut. The unknown cousins sharing in the windfall of the inheritance, the books shut on it and everything serene. And *finis* to the little puzzle of Robert Kinsolving. He looked at the few notes he had taken and felt tired thinking of what had to be done now. It looked like an impossible tangle, and it would probably just lead to a dead end, but before it did, it was going to mean a lot of work. He asked, "Could you give me the address where they were living then?"

"Yes, of course. Did I say it was Serrano Avenue? They lived there till about twelve years ago, and then they got an offer to buy it, some big company putting up apartments. Real estate's gone sky-high, I suppose you know—they got a hundred thousand for it, for heaven's sake, and they'd only paid forty-two hundred. Bob invested the money for them, and they lived in an apartment after that, till they died. Joe went first four years ago, and then Etta a couple of years later. Oh, I just dread telling Shirley about all this, but I see she's got to know." She went to the door with him. "I can't exactly say I've enjoyed meeting you, Mr. Falkenstein," and some of her usual forthright manner was back. "You'll never be able to find out any more than I've told you, it's a waste of time to think you can. And what does it all matter now?"

"Well, I'll have to try," said Jesse. But behind the wheel of the Mercedes he sat and swore aloud before he switched on the ignition. What a hell of a tangle, he thought. The small mystery of Robert Kinsolving had turned into a deeper mystery with a vengeance, a mystery in all probability to be left unsolved and insoluble. And it was nearly six o'clock, but Nell wasn't a worrier. He took the freeway back to Hollywood and drove down to Serrano Avenue, found that address. Forty-two years ago central Hollywood would have been a rather provincial town, its main business still the movie business, just starting to sprawl out into big city as the war brought more population flocking in. He slid the Mercedes into the curb. He could nearly see, in his mind's eye, the kind of house that had once occupied this lot then, a modest frame or stucco house, a little way back from the sidewalk. Now there were only three single houses left on this block, and they were old, shabby, dilapidated-looking. The rest of the block, including this lot, was filled with new smallish apartment buildings with garishly painted front doors and flimsy balconies. The narrow old street needed repaving, and a scattering of Mexican children were playing ball in the front yard across the street, chattering loudly in Spanish. He made a U-turn and headed back uptown, and, caught in the home-going traffic, he didn't get home to the house on Paradise Lane for forty minutes.

"But, Jesse," said Nell, "it's impossible." She had listened to the tale absorbedly over dinner. "Forty-two years, it'd just be impossible to find out anything about it now. And I certainly agree with Aunt Janet, there's nothing fair about it. The man wanted his sister to have everything—well, he thought she was his sister—and even if you could track down some blood relatives, it's not right that it should go to them—perfect strangers to him. If any. But you'd never find out anything."

"A few places to start looking," said Jesse. "The mother might have married, there could be half brothers and sisters. For pretty damn certain there's got to be a birth certificate on record."

"But how would you ever know which was the right one? It's the wild blue yonder," said Nell.

"Yes, I'm all for the clear shining truth coming out, but I could indeed wish that Aunt Janet had just kept quiet about this," said Jesse rather savagely. "What a damned mess! And I can see some of the money getting spent on trying to find out the rest of the truth. If that's possible at all."

"I just don't see where you could ever begin."

"Oh, a few things to try. Damn it, it just shows you how shortsighted people can be when it comes to the law. Putting off making wills. Afraid to put through the legal adoption for fear Big Brother could snatch the precious baby away. And that's one thing. It's remotely possible that they did adopt him legally later on, and I'd better find out about that. I should doubt it very much, on a couple of grounds. Aunt Janet would probably have heard about it, and if Kinsolving had been over five or six, he'd probably have been aware of it—the attorney would have had to see him. No, maybe a kid that age wouldn't have paid much attention. I'll have to look just to be sure. If there was an adoption, it'll be plain sailing, back to where we were. But I don't think there was. They would have told Aunt Janet, who'd urged them to do that when they took him. It's a mess all right, not least for the Grants."

"All that money," said Nell. "Probably ending up in Sacramento and getting squandered by the politicians."

"I know, I know," said Jesse testily. "If it comes to that, I'd rather spend some of it trying to trace him back than hand it over to those fellows."

"But it just occurred to me, even if he had signed that will, it wouldn't have been legal, would it? He wasn't Robert Kinsolving at all. Nobody knows who he was."

"Certainly it would have been legal, he was Robert Kinsolving. You can call yourself whatever you please, it's no crime to use a different name unless you're doing it in furtherance of a crime. Look at all the film stars who get born Mike Muggs and turn into Percy DeVere. Your name is the one you're known by to everyone who knows you. He'd been Robert Kinsolving all his life, that's who he was. Even if he'd signed the will, and this had come out later, it would have been a legal will."

"Oh, I didn't know that," said Nell.

"And something else. He'd been exempted by the Army—he'd never had a job or been in a situation where he had to show a birth certificate. I wonder whether they ever had one for him. Probably not. Well, the law's got some funny quirks, but on the whole it's aimed at justice and truth. Which in this case I rather wish it wasn't," said Jesse.

The Gordons had heard something about Kinsolvings, not much. On Tuesday morning they listened to the full tale and looked at him incredulously. They said simultaneously, "But it's impossible!"

"Difficult," said Jesse.

"You don't mean you think you can find out anything now?" asked Jean. "Forty-two years!"

"Well, it's not exactly back to the Dark Ages," said Jesse. "There are things to try, we may get lucky. The first thing to do, and I'll do it, is to call Sacramento and ask about a possible adoption." All the records on that would have been transferred to the state capitol from the individual counties. "They're not balls of fire up there, but when we can give them the name, they should be able to tell us yes or no pretty soon. But that's a very long shot and we'll do it just to be thorough." He lit a new cigarette and leaned back in his desk chair, looking out at the panorama of the smoggy city spread out below. "Meanwhile, one of you can chase down to the main library and start looking at city directories. All the old ones—they'll be in the archives. You know what to look for."

"Those neighbors," said Jimmy. "The Crossleys. Did you say Simon?"

"That's right. We don't know how long they lived at that address, when they died, or who the relative was who knew about the baby—who was going to have the baby. But if they had any family, somebody might know. Somebody still alive. Keep looking. The Crossleys owned the house, so Aunt Janet thought, and he'll be listed as the householder. You'll have to go through every directory from forty-two years back, until you find a break—one where he isn't listed. They were older than the Kinsolvings, so if you find him missing from a directory when he'd been in previous ones, it could pinpoint when he died. He or the wife."

"Or they could just have moved," said Jean pessimistically, "gone to live with a married daughter or into a nursing home."

"Don't be negative," said Jesse. "When you find them off the list of householders, then you go down to the county clerk's office and start looking for the record of a will made by either of them and probated that year."

"You were just saying," said Jimmy, "not everybody makes wills."

"We've got to go by the probabilities, it's all we can do," said Jesse. "Aunt Janet didn't remember how many children they had. Do you want to gamble that there was a son and start phoning all the Crossleys in all six phone books in case he's still here?"

"Oh, please," said Jean.

"Well, it was just a suggestion. The chances are, if they had a daughter, she's married. And forty-two years—people do move around. But we have to look, and that's the first place."

"Lord, what a job," said Jimmy. "At least you haven't got any appointments today. I don't suppose you'd feel inclined to come to the library with me and share the looking?"

"I've got something else to do. Go along, the sooner you start the sooner you'll be finished. And at least wills are on record right here. And the library's open until 9 P.M."

"If you expect either of us to do that much overtime, we go on strike, Mr. Falkenstein. We've got a double date tonight. If I don't develop migraine looking at all the directories. If they've got them all at the main library."

"They'll all be somewhere," said Jesse, "one library or another." She just gave him an eloquent look and went to get her handbag. She came back to look at her twin.

"If I don't find anything, you can take over tomorrow."

Jesse got up. "You hold down the fort," he said to Jean. "I'll be back sometime." He rode downstairs and got into the Mercedes, switching on the air-conditioning with the engine, and turned up Wilshire to Fairfax Avenue. The only public lot in the block he wanted was full; he had to park a block away. He climbed uncarpeted stairs in the shabby old building and went down a narrow corridor to a glass-fronted door labeled Thomas Garrett Associates, Private Investigations.

"Mr. Garrett in?" he asked the receptionist. "Tell him it's Falkenstein, I've got a job for him."

In a minute she came back and said, "You can come right in, sir."

Garrett, bigger and broader than ever, was lounging at his battered desk in the rear inner office. "What can we do for you, Mr. Falkenstein?"

"Well, if you're going to understand what I'm after, you'll have to listen to a story and I'd just as soon not tell it twice. I'll want at least one man, and if you've got anybody free and he's here, we'd better fetch him in."

"I think Allen's just finished up something." Garrett went to the door. "Gil in, Linda?"

"Yes, sir, in the main office."

"Shoot him in."

In a minute Allen came in, a smallish alert terrier of a man. "Oh, Mr. Falkenstein. You got something new for us?"

"Quite something," said Jesse. "I'll tell you about it." They all sat down and he launched into the tale.

When he came to Aunt Janet's revelation, Allen said, "Oh, brother. I know some law, I see where you're heading."

At the end Garrett asked, "Well, exactly where do you want to start?"

"Sacramento. Allen can fly up there right away and start the hunt tomorrow. Looking at birth certificates."

"All on microfilm," said Allen, and sighed. "And how the hell do I tell which is the right one?"

"You don't," said Jesse tersely. "We don't even have an exact date. His birthday was supposed to be November 1, but it might have been any day a week before or a week after, say. All we know is that he was supposedly just a few days old when the Kinsolvings took him. We know he was presumably illegitimate, and that'll show on the birth certificate."

"Brother," said Allen. "But would it? It was wartime, remember? There was a baby boom. Just how many babies do you think might have got born just in that two weeks, in the whole state? So we know he was born in California, when he was handed over just a little while later. That's about all we do know."

"I wouldn't guess how many."

"And would it show on the certificate that he was a bastard? Wartime, people flocking in here, soldiers, people after jobs in the defense plants. If the girl called herself Mrs. John Smith and said her husband was overseas, who was to doubt her? Hospitals don't ask to see marriage licenses."

"Well, that's the job," said Jesse. "You collect all the names on all those records, every boy baby born in that period of time, those two weeks. Check in with me and let me know where you're staying—it's possible I may turn up something to pin it down closer." He got out his checkbook. "You ought not to need more than four or five days at it."

"Me you have to wish it on," said Allen. "Okay, I'll get on it." He took the check with a nod. "I'll see if there's an afternoon flight, with any luck get in an hour's work today. The state offices close at six."

"If you need any more expenses, just ask."

Allen lifted a hand and went out. Garrett was filling an old pipe.

"You do run into the offbeat things, Falkenstein. At least these days there are the records to look at, all the tabs the nosy government keeps on the citizens. Where are you going to look besides the city directories?"

"That's about the only other line I can see at the moment," said Jesse. "I just hope to God those Crossleys had some relatives who are still alive. They're probably both dead by now. Relatives we can locate. It was some relative who knew the girl. Forty-two years, my God."

Garrett puffed on the pipe. "A hell of a long time. A lot of water under the bridge. People forget things that happen that long ago."

"Well, the circumstances were fairly unusual," said Jesse dryly. "There weren't nearly as many illegitimate babies then as there are these degenerate days. And the baby was just handed over without any formalities. Whoever arranged that won't have forgotten about it, whether it was the girl or the Crossleys' relative."

"And whoever that was might also be dead now too. I don't think you're going to come up with anything useful on this one. What the hell could you do with the birth records? My God, there must have been hundreds of kids born just that two weeks, in the whole state."

"Well, we look first at those born in Los Angeles County. Though it could have been anywhere in the state. When we've got a list of those illegitimate births, start looking for the mothers. I'll probably want another operative then. Look at marriage records, find out if any of those women got married later. Look up those names in the city directories."

"All over the damned state?" asked Garrett derisively. "You said yourself, people move around. The girl could have been from out of state, gone back home later. Gone somewhere else. I was just a kid, but I remember something about that time. Girls getting married and following soldier husbands all over. Girls coming out to work in the defense plants. Everything booming, everybody interested in the war. And all those USO clubs. This girl, whoever she was, I can see her just vanishing, leaving no record behind. After she had the baby, she could have got married, sure, but not necessarily here. She could also have gone anywhere in the country, she could have had the baby under a phony name, and there'll be no way on God's earth to locate her now. And," he grinned through a cloud of smoke, "in the very damned unlikely event that you did find her, had it occurred to you what her reaction might be? If you rang her doorbell and said, 'Excuse me, didn't you give birth to a bastard child forty-two years ago?' By now she might be, probably is, a respectable old lady with a legal husband and a grown-up family."

"There is that," admitted Jesse. "But as you say, water under the bridge since then. I should think the prospect of an unexpected tidy inheritance might take the sting out of it." After a moment he added suddenly, "And it'd be damned ironic, wouldn't it, if all those nice assets Kinsolving had accumulated should get passed on to the mother who gave him away like a stray kitten."

"You won't find her," said Garrett.

"I'm not taking any bets either," said Jesse. "But I've got to look. I'd almost rather see any individual get it than those greedy politicians."

"Oh, I'll agree with you there," said Garrett sardonically.

Jesse drove back to the office, and Jean told him a new client had just called for an appointment. A woman contemplating divorce. "Country going to the dogs," said Jesse. "All these broken marriages." It was eleven-thirty and probably all those state employees up there took a two-hour lunch break. Presently he went out to lunch himself, and it wasn't until one-thirty that he got on the phone to the appropriate records office in

Sacramento and talked to someone about the possible adoption. It was a female, and she sounded competent.

"I'd like to know as soon as possible whether there was an adoption filed. It's a matter of inheritance."

"I see. We can check that for you, of course. Would you spell that name again? Thank you. You don't have any date?"

"It probably wasn't a closer date than thirty-five years ago, if there was one." If it had been done after that, Kinsolving would have known about it. But he doubted very strongly that a record would show; he was just being cautious.

Jimmy trailed in at five o'clock and said bitterly, "They could use some better janitor service in that library basement. Look at my hands—the place is filthy with dust. I don't think anybody's looked at those old city directories in years. They were all over the place. Every time I finished with one I had to get a librarian to find the next one, and it took ages. I've only got up to thirty years ago. Oh yes, he was there. Listed as the house-holder at that address."

"Good," said Jesse.

"They're still there as far as I'm concerned, at least as far as I got. He was also listed as owning a piece of property on Western," and she added the address. "Up to thirty-eight years ago, and then that disappeared from the list. They, or he, was still living at the Serrano address thirty years ago. And I am beat. I want a long shower and something cold to drink. And if Tom and Rich want to go out dancing, they can think again."

Jesse waved them both off. "Go home and get all gussied up for your dates, girls. And have a good time."

He took off after them, and out of idle curiosity drove out Western to that address. The city had changed in those years, but there were still a lot of old buildings here and there. At that address far down on Western, nearly to the border of Hawthorne, there was a small garage with a smaller parking lot at one side. There was a sign over the garage door, Foreign Car Repairs. It was an old frame structure and could well have been here for all those years and more. Jesse parked in the lot, which contained a couple of Toyotas and an aged Volkswagen, and went in.

There was just one man in the place, bent over the open hood of a Subaru wagon. He looked about fifty, he was fat and bald and genial, ready to talk about anything without asking a reason. "Well, I've been here for nearly twenty-five years," he told Jesse. "Before that I had a place up on

Vermont, but when the rent shot up, it cut into the profits, and about then my dad died and left me this property, so I moved. Dad had used it for his business, he did furniture upholstery and refinishing, but it was easy enough to convert it. Parking lot ain't so big, but at least there is one."

"How long had your father owned it?"

He thought. "My God, it was years. Must have been around thirty-eight years ago he bought it—it was during the war or maybe just after. It was a printing shop when he bought it." He didn't ask why Jesse was interested, accepted a cigarette, and said he'd just been about to close up and go home. Following Jesse out, he said, "That's a damn beautiful set of wheels you're driving, mister. They're nice cars."

Jesse got home at six-forty to meet Fran just getting into her car at the curb. She had the baby with her, black-haired Miss Elaine sweetly and soundly asleep in her carrying crib. "I've got to fly, Jesse, I just woke up to what time it is, Nell and I got talking. I'm simply fascinated by this queer Kinsolving thing. Andrew'll be interested. But I don't see how you could possibly find out anything about it now." She blew him a kiss and switched on the engine. "Heavens, Andrew'll be home before I am, and I haven't any idea what to fix for dinner."

On Wednesday he talked to the new client about the divorce, and had another long argument on the phone with Mrs. Huff's attorney. Jean had taken over at the main library today and came in just as he got back from lunch. "Well, I found the break, and it gives us a sort of date, if it's just the year. Crossley stopped being listed at that address twenty-four years ago."

"Um, yes," said Jesse. "He retired and sold the printing business thirty-eight years ago. Probably he died sometime the year before he's missing from the directory."

"So now you can go and find out if he left a will," said Jimmy, "and I wish you joy of it. All the microfilm records at the county clerk's office."

"Yes," said Jesse. "And the sooner you start—"

"I know, I know," said Jean. "You know, you can be a slave driver sometimes. Let me go and have lunch first, for goodness' sake. And without a date it'll mean looking at all the wills filed over about eighteen months, and there'll be thousands. Don't rush me, I'll get there."

Allen called him on Thursday evening. "Just checking in, Mr. Falkenstein. This is one hell of a job. Just like I said, wartime and the baby boom. I've only scratched the surface. So far, I've got just two illegitimate births in that period. I don't know how long this is going to take me—I don't know if you want to run the bill up any higher. And another thing, he needn't have got put down as a bastard. Just like I said, hospitals don't ask for marriage licenses."

"Just keep at it," said Jesse resignedly. "Do you need some more expenses?"

"Not for a few days. I'll let you know. It's your money. But you sure as hell landed us with a sweet job this time. All this microfilm—I'll probably have to see an eye doctor by the time I get back."

And it wasn't Jesse's money, or wouldn't be in the end. It was Robert Kinsolving's lucky and shrewd investments piling up over the years that was going—could you call it poetic justice?—to try to trace him back to where he'd come from, what woman had borne him, who he'd been. In spite of what he'd said to Nell about the law, thought Jesse, sitting there with his hand still on the phone, there were times when the law was indeed an ass. Aunt Janet had gone straight to the truth of it. Kinsolving had been Kinsolving; the people who had taken him in and brought him up to be the steady good man he was had been more important to him than his natural parents. It was damned absurd on the face of it that the letter of the law should hold that, just because they hadn't signed the papers and filed the legal adoption away in the records, the money he'd left behind should belong to those anonymous—and probably unfindable —blood relatives, instead of the people he'd loved and thought of as his family. But that was how it was laid out, and as an honest man Jesse was bound to uphold the law, whether he agreed with it or not.

Nell was sitting up in bed reading a tome entitled *An Encyclopedia of Murder*. Jesse prodded Athelstane up and said, "Come on, monster, you've got to take a run before bed." Athelstane went out reluctantly; ten minutes later Jesse let him in again and went upstairs to undress. Nell had put her book down and was yawning.

"I don't know, Jesse. Sarah's really sort of ordinary. I'm back to thinking it's Esther."

Jesse grinned at her. "You're borrowing trouble. It's a fifty-fifty chance, and when you're so set on a female, it's bound to be another boy. Twins, triplets."

"Oh, for heaven's sake, don't try to be funny. That's all we'd need."

And as he undressed, he thought about those adoption agencies all that while back. So particular about matching the babies to the adoptive parents. The scientific ideas changed, and who was to say for the better or worse? These days they preached that environment was everything. Tomorrow they might be saying the opposite. He went down the hall to the bathroom and on the way back looked in on Davy, who was wrapped in innocent slumber with his favorite stuffed cat under one arm. Perhaps inevitably one of Solomon's proverbs slid into his mind: *Love covereth all sins.*

On Friday morning the records office in Sacramento called him, collect as instructed, and informed him that there was no record of an adoption on file for anyone named Kinsolving. He wasn't surprised; it was only confirmation of what he knew.

He had two divorce hearings coming up next week, and three new wills to draw up. There was always new business coming along.

At five-thirty Jimmy came in and announced, "Well, I found it finally. All that microfilm—it's murder. It was the year before Crossley turned up missing from the directory. He left a will, it was probated in October of the previous year. Twenty-four years ago. Evidently his wife was already dead—at least there wasn't any mention of her—and he'd made the will just a year before."

"Probably after she died," said Jesse. "What was in it?"

"He left everything to his daughter, a Mrs. Julia Severson. Her address was on Delmar Avenue in Hollywood."

"Well, a little step further on—thanks so much." He looked up the street in the county guide; it was above Franklin in the Hollywood Hills.

And it was time he did a little work on this himself. He brought Nell up to date over dinner, and about seven-thirty he drove out there and found Delmar Avenue, found the house. This was an old and good area of residential homes, if no longer exactly fashionable, and the one he wanted was a big sprawling Spanish stucco place with a red-tiled roof. The woman who opened the door was about forty, plump and blond. "I'm looking for a Mrs. Julia Severson." This wouldn't be her.

"Oh," she said rather blankly. "I'm Mrs. Wheeler. Well, yes, Mrs. Severson used to live here. We bought the house from her a year ago. She was a very old lady, I guess by what the daughter said she'd got so she couldn't take care of herself any longer, and her daughter—she was the one we talked with about the house—she said the old lady had to go into a nursing home. We never saw Mrs. Severson, she'd already moved out when we bought the house. It was her daughter showed us over the place."

"Do you remember her name?" asked Jesse.

"Good heavens, no. I'm sorry. No, of course I wouldn't have any idea what nursing home the old lady was in. We only met the daughter that once—we dealt with a realty company after that. Did you want to see Mrs. Severson about something important?" She looked at him curiously.

"A legal matter," said Jesse. And this looked like a very dead end, but there were still things to try on it. The Gordons weren't going to thank him for the next job he would hand them.

CHAPTER FIVE

"All the nursing homes in the county?" said Jean incredulously. "Do you have any idea how many there are? Thousands! It'll take a month of Sundays, and if she was an old lady a year ago, she could be dead, and those places are mostly big and impersonal, nobody would remember her. The things you think of for us to do."

"It's the next place to look," said Jesse. "And you can do it on the phone. Of course, there's no way of guessing which one it was, or is. It's probable that the daughter put her into one fairly near where she's living, and we don't know where she lives."

"Honestly," said Jimmy, "and there are those wills to get copied, and Mrs. Gorman's coming in to sign that codicil. We can spell each other, an hour on and an hour off." And that was on Monday morning, and Jesse had to be in court by ten. He left Jean starting the phone work and Jimmy typing and put it out of his mind to cover a divorce hearing. The judge was late in convening court and that took the rest of the morning. The girls hadn't come up with Mrs. Severson in any nursing home by the end of the day, and glancing at the list of those places just in the Central phone book, he wasn't surprised. He hadn't heard another word from Allen.

The week dragged on with the usual business. One old client came in to redraft his will, and another to put his house in joint tenancy after marrying a new wife. They were into August, and as was expectable the first heat wave had gone away temporarily, but would be back next month and worse.

By Thursday noon Mrs. Severson hadn't shown up at any of the nursing homes, and there were still a lot of them to check. It was a big county.

Jesse came back to the office that afternoon to find Gil Allen waiting for him in the client's chair, sitting back with his eyes shut smoking a cigarette. In the middle of the desk blotter was a stack of loose pages. "So there you are," said Allen, and stabbed a finger at the stack. "And what the hell can you do with it? Five hundred and seventy-nine, I counted them."

"My good God," said Jesse, looking at the top page. It was a neat typed list of names, dates, places.

"You've got no idea what a job that was," said Allen. "Look, I'm sorry if I wasted time and money on it, Mr. Falkenstein, but if you're going to do a thing, you've got to be thorough at it. It's all very well to say the right one would have got registered as a bastard, but it might not have, so I got them all. I weeded out all the girls, and all the blacks, of course—if they'd got added in it would have more than doubled that list and all the girl babies maybe doubled it again. Anyway, there they are, every white boy baby born in the state that two weeks. There are fifty-one of them listed as illegitimate, father unknown or a different name than the mothers."

"Good God," said Jesse faintly.

"And of all those, the illegitimate ones, there are twenty-one born in L.A. County. I suppose you want to start there first."

"It's the logical place to start," said Jesse.

Allen shut his eyes again. "You know that we'll get nowhere on it. Go look at marriage records for these names, up to forty years back or so, and even if we find any of these women listed, how the hell could we locate them now? Only householders get listed in the city directories, and not everybody's listed in the phone book. And anybody here forty years ago might be anywhere else by now, Florida or Indiana or New York."

Jesse contemplated the stack of paper and nearly shuddered. "We've gone this far, we'd better not stop now."

"More microfilm, at the county clerk's office," said Allen. "Hell and damnation. You'd better get a second operative on it if you expect anything to show very soon."

"Start with those twenty-one here, obviously," said Jesse. "I'll call Garrett. Thanks, Allen. I know what a hell of a job this must have been."

"I had to hire a typist to get it made up—that'll show up on the bill. I've got a Xerox of the list. I haven't been back to the office yet, I just flew in an hour ago."

"You can get started again tomorrow," said Jesse. "I'll get you some help."

Allen stood up and stretched. He looked tired and glum. "A hell of a lot of work and nothing to show for it, that's all I can see. But you're the boss. Right now I'm going home to see if my wife remembers what I look like." He went out, and Jesse reached for the phone and called Garrett.

Garrett was amused, hearing about the list. "I might have expected even more. You're just a damn fool to waste money like this. Do you really think you could turn up the right girl after all this time?"

"As long as we've got the damned list, we have to go on trying," said Jesse, annoyed. "I want somebody else to help out Allen."

"Throwing money away," said Garrett. "I can put Mary Lester onto it."

"Fine," said Jesse, remembering Mary Lester, whom he had liked when she had done a job for him earlier this year: a poker-faced dark-haired woman in her forties, attractive and efficient.

"I'll brief her on it," said Garrett, "and Allen will be in tomorrow with that list. But you know it's all going to come to nothing in the end."

"Never say die," said Jesse. "We don't know until we try."

"If you say so, you're the one laying out the money. They'll check in with you if anything turns up."

Jesse put down the phone and Jimmy came in with the mail. "He was late, he always is on Thursdays. I've finished my latest stint on the phone and Jeanie's taken over. We've just got through the Central book, we're up to the C's in the second one. I wouldn't have believed there were that many convalescent homes around. I suppose it's all the medical progress."

"Medical progress?" asked Jesse absently.

"People living longer and having to go into the convalescent homes," said Jimmy. "And I don't know that you can call it progress at that—it must be a sort of living death. We had an old aunt in one of those places, she died last year. And those places—all the old people just sitting around waiting to die—it's pathetic and horrible."

Jesse looked at the mail, which contained nothing of interest, and thought about the money pouring out to Garrett, and wondered if he was a damned fool to go on with this. But having put his hand to the plow, so to speak, maybe he hadn't any choice. And then Jimmy came back to say that another new client had just called in for an appointment, and would be in tomorrow morning. A Mr. John Olson, and he hadn't said what he wanted. "I'll be hearing," said Jesse. "Have you got Jenner's will copied yet?"

"I'll have it transcribed in another half hour."

"In that case, you'd better call him and tell him to come in and sign it."

What Olson wanted was a partnership contract, and he brought his prospective partner with him. They were about to embark on a con-tracting business. Jesse spent an hour with them on Friday morning, and after an early lunch went down to the Central Court for another divorce hearing. It took up most of the afternoon. And he almost decided to go straight home when it was finished, but on second thought went back to the office to see if anything new had showed up. Nothing had, and neither Allen nor Mary Lester had called in; it was too early to expect anything from either of them. He hadn't anything immediate to do except to dictate that contract to one of the girls, and at the moment he didn't feel inclined to get on with it. He sat idly staring out the window, thinking about the Kinsolving thing. Presently Jimmy put through a call, and it was Clock. "Fran's been telling me about the Kinsolving thing. And a damn funny one that is, Jesse, and if you ask me it's just one damn shame about all the money. I'm sworn to uphold the law, but sometimes the law doesn't make much sense, does it? All the money going to strangers or the state, depending on what you turn up or don't. And for God's sake, how you could ever trace him back now, I don't see. Have you found out anything else?"

"The number of white boy babies born in the whole state about the same time," said Jesse. "I don't know, Andrew, the way it's looking now I'm thinking the state's going to get the windfall."

"Well, I'm damn sorry for those Grants," said Clock. "It's just a damn shame. And that whole business still worries me just a little—the way he died. For ninety-nine percent sure it was the typical suicide, but I wish I could feel a hundred percent sure. Just that little bit of residue showing up —of course, that silly little gun—"

"Well, there's nothing anybody can do about that now," said Jesse soberly. "But I know what you mean."

They kicked it around a little before Clock said, "Damn it, I'm goofing off. We're up to our ears in new heists, and there's another unidentified body. I'll see you sometime."

Jesse went on staring out the window, and after a while Jimmy came in and said, "It's quitting time. Jean's just got one more call to make to finish off the M's in the Valley book and then we'll take off." Jesse looked at his watch and discovered that it was five-forty.

"So I'll see you on Monday," he said.

In the outer office Jean suddenly uttered a small yelp and the next moment looked in the door. "I don't believe it, but we've got there, Mr. Falkenstein. Just now. It's the Morningside Convalescent Home in Pasadena. Mrs. Julia Severson's a patient there."

"Well, praise be," said Jesse.

"And what all that's going to do to the phone bill we'll be finding out," said Jean. "But thank God that job's over."

"Have a nice weekend, girls. You both deserve it."

Those places had evening visiting hours. If there was anything here to be got, he wanted to hear about it as soon as possible. He left Nell reading about Dame Wiggins of Lee to Davy before bed, and found the Morningside Convalescent Home on a secondary main drag in Pasadena. It was a big old stucco building, with a couple of wings added on, and its own parking lot. He went into a small front anteroom with a counter on the rear wall, several doors leading off it in several directions. It was empty, apparently not a soul around, and he was debating about trying one of the doors when a white-uniformed nurse popped up behind the high counter and said, "Can I help you, sir?"

"Mrs. Julia Severson," said Jesse. "I understand she's a patient here. Could I see her?"

She was a little thin woman with strawberry blond hair. She said, "Well, let me see." She consulted a list posted on the wall behind her desk. "That'll be Annex A. Through that door, and ask for Miss Tally at the nurses' station."

Obediently he went down a long corridor covered in polished linoleum, passed a lot of room doors, and came to a nurses' station at the far end. There were four uniformed nurses sitting there. "Miss Tally?" One of them looked up, a thin dark woman about forty with a long nose and a thin-lipped mouth. "I'd like to see Mrs. Severson," and he handed her a card.

She looked up at him rather blankly, looked at the card. "What's it about? You're a lawyer?"

"She may possibly have some information I need, I've spent quite a time trying to find her."

She looked at the card again, looked back at him, and said, "Well, if that's so, I'm sorry, sir, but I'm afraid she couldn't be of any help to you at all. She's nearly completely senile—her mind's just a blank and she hardly ever speaks, and then not to make any sense. She has to be cared for like a baby, you know how some of them go. She wouldn't understand any questions—she doesn't even recognize her own daughter now."

So that was that, thought Jesse. "There's a daughter?"

"Yes, she comes in regularly to check up, but this is a good place and she's getting good care—Mrs. Severson, I mean. Well, Mrs. Morgan at the front desk could give you her address—she's the next of kin, of course. Poor old soul, the doctor thinks she might go at any time, and it'd be a mercy if she did. She's eighty-six and just skin and bones. And of course a job to take care of, but that's what we're here for."

Feeling discouraged, Jesse plodded back to the front anteroom and asked questions. The strawberry blond consulted a book on her desk and said briskly, "It's Mrs. James Pryor, Oakwood Street."

Back in the car Jesse consulted a city map. Oakwood Street was right here, in upper Pasadena. He found the street, found the house, which was a big handsome Spanish place in a block of equally opulent-looking houses. There were lights showing and he went up to the porch and pushed the bell. In a few moments the door opened and he faced a goodlooking young woman in a turquoise-blue pants suit. She had reddish brown hair, a pert tip-tilted nose, and a wide friendly mouth. "I'd like to see Mrs. Pryor."

"Oh, they're not home, I'm sorry," she said. "They're on vacation in Honolulu. I'm just the cat-sitter, I'm Stephanie Keene. They don't go away very often, but when they do, I stay to take care of the cats while they're gone. I'm his secretary, Mr. Pryor's."

Well, it was August, when a lot of people went off on vacation. "When do you expect them back?" he asked.

"They're supposed to be back on Thursday. Well, they'd better be—he's got that big lawsuit coming up in court on Friday. They ought to have arranged to get back earlier—he won't be fit for a big case so soon. I know him," said the cat-sitter darkly, "and he'll have been out all day swimming and surfing, and for goodness' sake, he was sixty last month, but try to talk to a man."

Jesse suppressed a grin and handed her a card. "It's Mrs. Pryor I want to talk to."

"Oh, you're a lawyer too," she said, scanning the card. "What's it about?"

"She may be able to give me some information I need. Tell her I'll be in touch with her as soon as she's home. Or she can call me."

"All right, I'll tell her." She was curious, but as an evidently well-trained legal secretary didn't ask any more questions. "They're supposed to be back about noon on Thursday."

Well, he thought, sliding behind the wheel, preserve the soul in patience.

What looked like a first jackpot showed up on Tuesday afternoon, and it was Mary Lester who turned it up. For three days she and Gil Allen had been pouring over the microfilm at the county clerk's office downtown, looking at old marriage licenses, and she hadn't expected to come across anything relevant that soon.

She liked that nice Mr. Falkenstein, and he'd given them a few interesting jobs to do before, but she had her private reasons for feeling particularly interested in this one. She liked working for Garrett Associates; she'd held various jobs in the course of her life, and she was efficient at office work, but she detested it, preferring something that got her out and about more, and this job certainly did that.

She and Allen had started out first with that list of the twenty-one names, the twenty-one girls or women who had given birth to illegitimate baby boys sometime during that two-week period forty-two years ago, in L.A. County. One of them had been named Rose Vogel, and just after Mary had got back from lunch on Tuesday and settled down with the microfilm viewer again, she came across a marriage license with Rose Vogel's name on it. It was dated thirty-five years back, a license issued to Rose Vogel and Alfred Sadler. She took down the date and names, and went out to the front of the building where there was a rank of public phones. In the official building belonging to the city all six phone books were available. In the third one she consulted, she found an Alfred Sadler listed at an address in Burbank. She dialed the number and on the fourth ring a woman answered.

"Mrs. Sadler?"

"Yes, who is this?"

"Was your maiden name Rose Vogel?"

"Why, yes. Who is this and what do you want?"

Mary introduced herself politely. "I'm doing some work for a lawyer, Mrs. Sadler. We're trying to get some information you might be able to give me. Would it be convenient if I came to see you now? I won't take up much of your time."

"Well, I guess so, but what's it about?"

"I'll explain when I see you, thank you."

She got on the freeway and over in Burbank found the address. It was a modest old stucco place on a quiet side street. The woman who opened the door looked about sixty, a nice-looking woman who had once probably been very pretty; she was neat in a plain cotton housedress, her gray hair slightly wavy in a short cut. She said curiously, "What's this all about? Oh, come in and sit down. You said your name's Lester?"

Mary sat down on the shabby couch. "It's about a baby," she said gently. "A baby boy born forty-two years ago in October, at the Hollywood Hospital." Sudden fright came into the other woman's eyes. "I don't want to frighten you, Mrs. Sadler, and nobody's going to talk about it or tell your family. But we're trying to trace a baby born about then. It's important that we find out about him, what happened to him, and it might have been your baby. It's a question of a legacy, and if it was your baby, the one we're trying to find out about, it might mean some money for you."

She was gripping the arms of her chair tightly. "I don't know what you mean," she said thickly.

"I think you do," said Mary quietly. "We've seen the birth certificate, you know, with your name on it and a Walter Johnson named as the father. I'm not going to bother you, no one's going to bother you, but we've got to find out what happened to the baby. Did you keep him, or give him up for adoption?"

After a long moment Mrs. Sadler said in a dull voice, "The birth certificate." She brought out a handkerchief and wiped her mouth with it. "So you know I had the baby, it was me. You asking my maiden name."

"Nobody wants to make any trouble for you, we just have to know what happened to the baby."

She hunched over in the chair, clutching the handkerchief. "That's all you want to know. If I tell you, you won't come here again or tell anybody?"

"That's right," said Mary.

She passed the handkerchief over her mouth again. "Not that I suppose it'd matter now," she said slowly. "My husband knows about it—I figured it was only honest to tell him before we got married. And he's a good man, he understood how things can happen. Our two girls don't know, no reason to tell them, but they're both sensible and they'd understand it too. And it was so long ago. You see, it was the war. You'd be too young to remember that, of course. It was the war. I was eighteen. Walt and I, we'd been going together for about a year—we were in high school together— and he got drafted into the Army. They sent him off for training some- where in Georgia, and then he came back on leave before he'd be going overseas. That was when it happened—the reason it happened. When I knew I was going to have the baby, I wrote and told him. And he'd have come back and married me if he could—we'd planned on getting married when he came back. But he was waiting to get shipped out and he couldn't get back. He sent me all the money he had, and he wrote me we'd get married as soon as he got back to America. My folks, they stood by me, they knew Walt, that he was a good man and we'd get married as soon as we could. But you see, he never got back home. He was killed some place in Italy before the baby was born. He'd put my name down to be notified, in case, and I got a telegram."

"I see," said Mary. "I'm sorry."

Mrs. Sadler was staring at the floor. "I thought I wanted to die too, right then. And I wanted to keep Walt's baby—it was all I had left. But my dad was sick then, he couldn't work for a long time, and there were all the doctor bills, and Mother had to stay home to take care of him. There were my doctor bills too. I hadn't had an easy time while I was carrying the baby, and I knew I'd have to get a job to help out. I couldn't take care of the baby."

"Did you give him up for adoption?"

"Myra was the only one who had a job, my older sister Myra, and money was pretty tight. No, I didn't do that, exactly the way you mean it. Myra, she knew some people who couldn't have any children of their own and wanted to adopt a baby. I don't even know their name. She and Mother said it was better I shouldn't know, so as to put it all behind me. I got out of the hospital three days after the baby was born, and Myra took him away right off. I didn't know where. I thought I'd die, giving Walt's baby away to strangers, to be theirs. You see, he didn't have any folks—he was an orphan and this old aunt had brought him up just because she had to, she was the only relative. She didn't really care much about him, and she wouldn't have cared about the baby at all. I came to see it was the sensible thing to do, but right then I couldn't stop crying about it. Giving Walt's baby away like that." Mrs. Sadler straightened up and put the handkerchief away. "But you get over things, you know. Time goes by and you get over things and stop thinking about them any longer. I got a pretty good job at Lockheed, and after the war I took a course in beauty work—that's what I was doing when I met Al, working at a beauty shop in Glendale. And somehow, well, I never forgot Walt, but he was gone, and kind of dim in my mind then. I was twenty-six—I'd got over it. You forget things. Al and I have been happy together, and we've got the two girls—they're good girls."

"Is your sister still alive?" asked Mary.

"Myra? Yes, she just lost her husband last year. She's living with her married daughter."

"It's a long time ago, Mrs. Sadler. And we have to know what happened to the baby. Just to know. Do you think, if you asked your sister, she'd tell me where she took the baby?"

Mrs. Sadler said, "Yes, it's a long time. I can't see that it'd matter now, after all these years. I can ask her. She lives right here in town. Do you want to see her?"

"Please," said Mary.

"Well, I'll phone her now, she's likely at home. She's got the arthritis pretty bad and doesn't go out much."

"I'm sorry to have brought it all back to you."

"It doesn't matter," said Mrs. Sadler. "You get over things."

Mary thought she'd give her time to talk it over with the sister, and drove back to a main street and found a public phone. She thought wryly that it was possibly the worst tragedy of life, that you forgot things. All the wild passions, the loves and hates—after a while it seemed as if they had all happened to someone else. Time passed, and you forgot. She called Mr. Falkenstein's office and one of his secretaries relayed the call.

"You won't believe it, Mr. Falkenstein, but I may have found the right one for you."

"Don't tell me. Already?"

"I know, it'd be the biggest fluke there could be, but it's possible." She told him all about it.

"Yes, it sounds very possible indeed, but what could it have to do with the Crossleys and the Kinsolvings?"

"There could have been a connection. The Janet woman was pretty vague, just said a relative or friend, she thinks. This sister could have known some relative of the Crossleys, heard about the Kinsolvings."

"Well, let me know what the sister has to say as soon as you hear."

"I'm just going to see her. I'll let you know."

The sister, whose name was Peck, lived in another modest stucco house on another side street. She was home alone, a rather dour-looking old lady a few years older than Rose Sadler, and she looked at Mary without much enthusiasm. "Yes, I've just been talking with Rose," she said. She hadn't asked Mary in. "She said I might as well tell you. I guess it couldn't matter now, nobody could make any trouble about it when it happened so long ago."

"Your sister said you knew some people who wanted to adopt a baby. Who were they, Mrs. Peck?"

She said reluctantly, "I was working in an office downtown then, when it happened, doing filing—it was a big title and loan company. One of the other girls there and I got friendly, her name was Isabelle Evans. She had a sister a good bit older than her, in her thirties, and she'd been married a long while, but they couldn't have children and they were trying to adopt a baby. I thought about it right off when we decided Rose couldn't keep the baby, and I talked to Isabelle about it. She took me to meet her sister, and she got all excited about it and said sure they'd take it. The husband was an electrician. They seemed like nice people, and they sure wanted the baby. Their name was Taylor."

Mary went back to the public phone and called Mr. Falkenstein's office again. It had, of course, been too good to be true, but she was feeling tired and discouraged. And by now it was too late to get back to the microfilm. She'd go home and have a long cool bath before dinner, and shampoo her hair and get to bed early.

Jesse had to be in court most of Thursday, and when he got back to the office at four-thirty, the Gordons told him there hadn't been any calls. He had rather expected that Mrs. James Pryor would have been curious enough to call and ask what he wanted of her. He got home early, and Davy monopolized him for the hour before dinner, insisting on being read to from the big book of nursery rhymes. Nell whisked him off to bed and they sat down to dinner, with Athelstane hopefully begging for handouts.

"Don't you give him anything," said Nell. "He's too fat now."

"And look who's talking." Jesse grinned at her. With a little less than three months to go, Nell was definitely bulging with the baby.

"Well, mine's not permanent," she said peacefully, and poured his coffee. "No more false alarms?"

"Not so far."

"You're never going to get anywhere on it, you know."

"You're probably all too right, but play it out to the bitter end. They've just got through the illegitimate babies down here and they're now looking at the ones born in adjacent counties."

"And they'll turn up nothing," said Nell. "Find out they were all legally adopted."

"It's a long job, we won't know for a while."

After dinner he went into the study, looked up the number, and dialed the Pryors' house in Pasadena. On the second ring he was answered by the cat-sitter. "Oh, you're the one who was here the other night. No, they're not back yet," and she sounded resigned. "That court case got postponed, and Mr. Pryor'd asked me to wire him if it did. He had a hunch it might be. So they decided to stay another couple of days. They're supposed to be getting back on Sunday now. Oh yes, I'll give her your card, I haven't forgotten."

On Friday, after a last long argument on the phone with Mrs. Huff's attorney, he got him to back down and agree to the offered settlement. Then he talked to Huff, who was still annoyed that he had to give her anything at all. "Business is lousy," said Huff, who was a realtor, "and that damned house is worth two hundred and fifty thousand as it stands, if I could sell it to anybody. Damn it, I'm paying three hundred a month for a crummy hole-in-the-wall apartment, and driving a seven-year-old heap that needs work, and she gets the house and the new car." He ended by sounding resigned. "Hell, I suppose I should just be thankful to be getting rid of her, the bills she was always running up. God, how that woman can spend money. When is it coming off?"

"It's all over but the shouting, Mr. Huff. Now she's accepted the settlement, we just have to wait for her attorney to get it on the court agenda. I should think it'd probably be sometime toward the end of the month."

"Well, all right. You'll let me know."

"You'll be hearing—you'll get the papers served on you."

"So thanks very much and good riddance," said Huff. "Now if the interest rates would just go down so I could make some sales—"

"Afraid that's out of my line," said Jesse.

Gil Allen called him that night from Santa Barbara to report that he'd cleared four more possible babies out of the running. One of them had been kept by the mother and the other three had been given up for adoption at the agency operated by the county. All of those would have been legally adopted in due course. "You're wasting quite a lot of money on this, Mr. Falkenstein. Want to call it off?"

"Maybe sometime. You keep plugging away awhile longer."

"I'm heading for San Luis Obispo tomorrow," said Allen. "And you can't really think that this girl lived up there, had the baby there, when she knew about the Kinsolvings down in L.A.?"

"We don't know, damn it," said Jesse. "It's all up in the air, anything's possible. You keep at it."

It was nine-thirty on Sunday night when he heard from Mrs. Pryor. She had a low pleasant contralto voice. "Is this the Mr. Falkenstein who wanted to see me about some legal business?" she asked after introducing herself.

"That's right, Mrs. Pryor."

"Stephanie gave me your card, but it just had the office number on it. I found you in the phone book. My curiosity's itching, and I decided not to wait until tomorrow. What is it you want with me, for goodness' sake?"

"Well, it's rather a long story to go into on the phone, Mrs. Pryor. Would it be convenient if I saw you at home tomorrow? In the afternoon?"

"Yes, that'd be all right. As Stephanie probably told you, we just got back from Hawaii today, but I can do the marketing in the morning."

"Say two o'clock?"

"Yes, that would be fine. You really have aroused my curiosity, Mr. Falkenstein."

Jesse laughed. "I just hope you might have some information I need, Mrs. Pryor. I'll see you tomorrow at two, then."

It had turned slightly cooler, and he didn't need the air-conditioning in the car. Next month and the month after, the real heat would arrive, the foretaste of hell that was Southern California in September and October, when the rest of the country was enjoying cool fall weather. Maybe the rest of the population was right in thinking there was something peculiar about Californians; only someone who had spent years in the Southern California climate could understand the fervent eagerness Californians felt for the onset of autumn, the possibility of cool weather and even some rain, while everybody back East was feeling apprehensive about blizzards and ice storms. As with a number of other things in life, it depended where you sat.

When he pulled up in front of the handsome big house and climbed the steps to the front porch, the door was standing open behind the ornamental screen door. The chimes had barely sounded before she appeared. "Mr. Falkenstein? Come in. I'm Lois Pryor." She was probably around sixty, but still attractive, with a nice slim figure in a tailored navy pantsuit, crisp curly silver-gray hair in a fashionable cut, discreet makeup, with a still-pretty youthful-looking face. She took him into a big cool living room a step down from the entrance hall, and for the first time he saw the cats: two large seal point Siamese sitting in an armchair, observing him interestedly. "Sit down," she said. "And for heaven's sake, tell me what this is all about. Jim was annoyed that he couldn't meet you, he's really not back to work yet but he had an appointment with a client to draw up a will."

"Wills," said Jesse. "It's a will that started all this business, Mrs. Pryor. A will that never got signed." He sat down on the couch, and one of the cats immediately came over and jumped up on his lap.

"Oh, I'm sorry, let me put her off. She goes to everybody—I hope you don't mind cats—"

"That's all right, leave her," he said, stroking the cat's ears. "We've got one of these too. What's her name?"

"Iris. I know it's a silly name for a cat. Her sister's Lily. Now what on earth is your business with me?"

"Well, it's a long tangled tale, and it goes back a way, Mrs. Pryor. I'll ask you first, Simon Crossley and his wife were your grandparents? Your mother's parents?"

She looked extremely surprised. "That's right, but they've been gone for years."

"Yes, I know. You see, I was looking for your mother first, and then when I found out which convalescent home she was in—" He paused.

Sadness came into her fine dark eyes. "It's terrible to see her like that, just barely alive. Not knowing anybody, even me or Jim. She was always so active and alert, and so fond of us and the children—We never thought she'd go like this. All we can do for her is to see she gets the best of care. And it's an awful thing to say, but we both hope she won't linger on, that she'll just fade away and go. And find Dad and all her friends somewhere again. She's eighty-six—it was only about two years ago she began to fail."

"Well," said Jesse, stroking the cat, who had begun to purr loudly, "your grandparents were living on Serrano Avenue in Hollywood forty-two years ago."

"Yes, that's right," she said.

"And next door to them lived some people named Kinsolving. Joseph and Etta Kinsolving. They were friends, even though the Kinsolvings were younger. They neighbored, in the colloquial sense of the word. Sometimes played cards together."

She was sitting in the chair opposite him, and her dark eyes were intelligent and interested. "The Kinsolvings, yes," she said. "What about them?"

"They wanted children and couldn't have any of their own, and about that time—forty-two years ago—they took a newborn baby boy. They're both dead now too, and the only one who knew anything about it was Kinsolving's younger sister. She told us that some friend or relative of the Crossleys knew a girl who was going to have a baby and wanted to give it up. You see, it's a question of a possible legacy. If it's at all possible, I've got to find out where that baby came from. Would you have any idea who

might have passed on that information—about the girl expecting the baby
—from your grandparents to the Kinsolvings?"

"Well, of all the queer things," she said. "After all this time. It's about
that? Of all the strange things—all this time after. But yes, I can tell you
that, Mr. Falkenstein. It was me."

CHAPTER SIX

"The hell you say!" Jesse was startled.

She smiled slightly. "Yes, I can tell you something about it. This is funny, all those years back, and you wanting to know about it now. Why do you want to know?"

Jesse told her the whole tale and she listened absorbedly. At the end she said soberly, "What a legal mess. My husband's a lawyer too, you know, and he's going to be very interested in this. Yes, I see what you're up against, and I'm afraid I can't take you much farther, but I can tell you something. I hadn't thought about that in years—well, it was a long time ago."

"Who was the girl, Mrs. Pryor?"

"I don't know," said Lois Pryor. "I never did know. It was a girl named Leila Gray who told me." He offered her a cigarette and she declined it. There was an ashtray on the coffee table and he lit one for himself. "I'll tell you just what happened. I was still in high school. You know there are two graduating classes every year, winter and summer, January and June. I was going to be graduating in June. Leila Gray had graduated in January. This was Fairfax High School, I should say—my parents and I were living on Curson Avenue in Hollywood. I didn't know Leila very well at all. We'd had a gym class together once and I just knew who she was, that's all. It was one of those desultory things. It was that May, and I was so surprised when she turned up that day at school. As I say, she'd been in the January graduating class. One day when I came out of the school grounds after my last class—I had to take the bus up on Melrose—she was there at the front gate, she grabbed my arm and said she wanted to talk to me. I was with a couple of other girls, I forget who, and she said it was something private, she had to talk to me alone. We sat on a bench in front of the school, and she said she remembered hearing me say something about some people who wanted to adopt a baby. I couldn't think what she meant at first, and then I remembered. It was one day in the cafeteria and we were talking—you know how girls that age do—about getting married and having families and how many children we'd like to have, and all that.

And I'd mentioned these people my grandparents knew who were so disappointed at not having children and couldn't get one to adopt. Grandma had been talking about it just recently. And Leila said she knew a girl who was going to have a baby and wanted to give it up, and she said she'd just remembered about my talking about these people, maybe they'd want the baby, and she asked who they were. Well, I was surprised. I didn't know what to do at first, but she kept on at me and finally I told her the name and address. Naturally I asked her who the girl was, and she just said never mind, it wasn't any of my business. But she thanked me, and she said she'd see the people and ask if they'd take the baby." Lois Pryor leaned back in her chair and gave a little sigh. "Life is funny," she said. "Which is a trite thing to say, but it is. I saw that baby once, you know. I think it was that Christmas—we were at Grandpa's and the Kinsolvings came over with him. They were so thrilled to have him, showing him off. He was a sweet baby. I'm sure they didn't know it was me who'd told Leila about them. They never mentioned it, and thinking it over, I think what probably happened was that Leila just told them it was somebody who knew Grandpa and Grandma who'd told her about them. And that could have been anybody, of course."

"Did you tell anybody about it?" asked Jesse.

"Well, I told Dad and Mother. I wasn't exactly sure I'd done the right thing. Mother said not to worry about it—if it meant those people could adopt a baby, it was the best thing for everybody concerned. She asked me if I knew who the girl could be and of course I didn't. Just some girl Leila knew. Of course, I was curious about it because I thought it was probably some girl in Leila's class, some girl at Fairfax too. But I couldn't get anything out of Leila that day. And I never saw her again. She was sort of —well, all business, sort of abrupt and gruff, if you see what I mean."

"I see," said Jesse. "So that was the connection. Yes, it almost had to be some girl at the same school. Unless it was Leila Gray herself."

"Oh no," said Lois Pryor. "It wasn't Leila. That was in May, as I said, and she told me the baby was due in late October. If that were so, the girl would have been about four months along and it would have showed, and Leila was thin as a rail. It wasn't her."

"She was just being helpful?" said Jesse. "If you can call it that. Remembered your mentioning the people who wanted to adopt a baby, and thought it might be a convenient place for her friend to dispose of the baby."

"I think that's what it amounted to," she said. "Naturally I was terribly curious because I thought I might know the girl, whoever she was. But as I

say, I never saw Leila again. The next thing I heard about it was when
Grandma told me how the Kinsolvings had taken a baby and how happy
they were about it. And then I saw the baby just that one time. That
Christmas. I'd graduated from high school in June, and I was going to
L.A. City College, and then the next January I transferred to USC. I
didn't get over to Grandpa's house very often, and it was usually evenings.
I don't remember seeing either of the Kinsolvings ever again."

"Well, that's all very interesting," said Jesse, "and it could take me a
little further, couldn't it? You've got no idea who the girl might have
been? Some friend of this Leila Gray's."

"And I didn't know her well at all. Just thinking back," said Lois Pryor,
"I didn't like her very much, what I do remember about her. She was"—
her nose wrinkled—"a little bossy, that type. So sure of herself, sure she
was right about everything. You know the kind."

"Yes," said Jesse. "Did you do any guessing about it?"

"Well, naturally I did." She laughed. "But it's a big school, and I didn't
know some of the girls Leila was friendly with, not well. I knew who they
were, generally speaking, but none of them were friends of mine. Oh, I
did some guessing all right, but there wasn't any way to know for sure.
And it's another funny thing, you know, you have some good friends in
school and you think that you'll go on being friends, but somehow after
you get out of school, you lose touch. You go on to different things and so
do they, and after a while you even forget most of their names. The only
one I've kept in touch with since high school is Betty Jo Chapman—well,
it's Canning now. Oh, of course I told her about it at the time, and a
couple of other girls, and we were all frantically curious about who it
might be, but there wasn't any way to know."

"Well, thanks very much," said Jesse. "At least we know now what the
contact was. And this Leila, if we can locate her, she knew who the baby's
mother was."

"And if you can locate her," said Lois Pryor, "if she's still around here
somewhere, she'd probably tell you. What I just said—yes, she was just
being helpful. Helping out a friend. But forty-two years ago—you lose
touch with people. The other girl, they might have been bosom friends
then and drifted away from each other years ago."

"That's so," said Jesse. "But she could tell us the name."

"All that money," she said. "It doesn't seem at all fair it might end up
going to the mother. After she just handed the baby over to strangers. But
if you ever find out, I'd be awfully interested to hear about it. And Jim's
going to be fascinated by all this. He was in the same graduating class, you

know. The one Leila was in. I'd told him about it at the time—Leila and the girl who was going to have the baby. We'd already been dating pretty steady. That is, I wrote him about it, he was in the Army then, up at Fort Ord. We got engaged the year after that, and then he went overseas, but not for long. We were married two years later, after the war ended, and that was a rough time." She smiled reminiscently. "Jim in law school and me working to keep the rent paid. But we got through all right. We couldn't start the family until four years after we'd got married."

"Well, all this gives me a definite place to go. Leila Gray. I'm much obliged, Mrs. Pryor."

"You've certainly brought back some memories, Mr. Falkenstein," and she smiled at him. "Jim will be sorry he missed you. He's going to be interested to hear all this."

As soon as Jesse got back to the office, he called Garrett. "What do you want now?" asked Garrett.

"Do you know where Mary Lester is?"

"Certainly, she's down in San Diego chasing your wild goose."

"Well, I think you'd better fetch her back. Leave Allen where he is for the moment, but we may be going to get a little break. At least we've now got a definite name to look for. The same routine, marriage licenses, city directories, phone books, but we know now what the connection was." He brought Garrett up to date on the latest news.

Garrett was interested. "That's very useful all right. If we can find this Leila Gray, bingo, she can tell us who the mother was. She may even be in contact with her. I'll get hold of Mary, she can probably get back sometime tomorrow. I never expected to get anywhere on this damned thing, but this looks encouraging."

The Gordons were interested too, but they were in agreement with everybody else on the probable outcome of it. "There's nothing right about it, if you find the mother and she gets the money," said Jean. "From the baby she gave away."

"He intended his sister to have it," said Jimmy, "and from what you said, she sounds like a nice woman, and she could use the money, with two young children and her husband a teacher. She and her brother were evidently pretty close, and it must have been bad enough for her, him committing suicide, without finding out he wasn't her brother and losing all the money too. It just doesn't seem fair. In a way, I hope we never do find that woman, Mr. Falkenstein. I'd almost rather see the money go to the state."

Jesse said mildly, "I'm spending some of it."

He got home a little early and told Nell all about it, and of course she agreed with the Gordons. "I never thought you'd get a clue, but if you can locate that Gray woman— And what a legal mess it's been, Jesse. It's just criminal to think of his money going to a woman like that. I'm sorry for Mrs. Grant."

"Yes, so am I," said Jesse, "but there's nothing to be done about it— there it is."

He was relaxing in his armchair over a peaceful drink while Nell was upstairs with Davy, when the phone rang at his elbow and he picked it up. "Mr. Falkenstein? This is Jim Pryor, I just missed you by fifteen minutes and Lois and I have been talking this thing over. You've got a real bastard of a job on this thing, haven't you? But I've got an idea we may be able to give you some help on it."

"Any advice gratefully accepted," said Jesse.

"I don't know why Lois didn't think of it when she was talking to you this afternoon," said Pryor. "We've got something that might be of use to you. Look, I can see what you're up against here. If you can track down this Leila Gray, she can tell you what girl had the baby, if she will. Whether you could ever find that one or not. But you might not be able to find her. Forty-two years is a hell of a long time. Or she could be dead. We've got something I think you'll want to see. Would it be all right if we came over this evening with it? Say eight o'clock."

"Fine," said Jesse.

"It's an interesting little legal tangle, and I'd like to meet you. Where are you and how do we get there?" Jesse told him. "Good," said Pryor. "We'll be there around eight."

Nell, coming back from getting Davy off to bed, was slightly annoyed. "Heavens, I haven't dusted or vacuumed all week, and the way you will scatter newspapers around— We'd better have dinner right away." She didn't let him dawdle over it, whisked the dishes into the dishwasher, and did some hasty straightening up in the living room.

"You'd better get Athelstane in before they come. About his only virtue, he does bark at strangers and he might scare Mrs. Pryor."

At this time of year it was still light at eight o'clock, and Jesse was waiting on the front porch to unlock the gates for them when they arrived. "Found us okay, good."

"You've got a big place here," said Pryor, offering his hand. "Quiet up here away from town, I'll bet." He was a big man, lean and young-looking for his age, with a deep tan. All the swimming and surfing, thought Jesse.

"Yes, we've got an acre, no close neighbors."

As they came up the front walk, Nell opened the door and Athelstane came bumbling out briskly. "Good heavens," said Lois Pryor, "is that a dog or a pony?"

"Mastiff," said Jesse. "Don't worry, he's something of an idiot." He introduced Nell as they came into the living room.

"Oh, what a beauty," said Mrs. Pryor, going to admire the sinuous elegance of the cat stretched out on the mantel. "What's her name?"

"He," said Nell, smiling. "Murteza. It means the lion of God in Arabic. Won't you sit down?"

They sat together on the couch, and Pryor took something from under his arm and laid it on the coffee table, a rather large book. "I don't know why Lois didn't think of this when she saw you this afternoon. God knows where my copy of it got to, but we still have hers."

"I hadn't thought of it in years," she said.

"Well, I did," said Pryor. "It's the class yearbook. We've been talking this over, and I think there are some definite conclusions you can draw." He was a very good-looking man, with strong regular features; he looked at Jesse keenly. "First of all, let's suppose you can't find Leila Gray. You've still narrowed the field some. We both think, whoever the girl was, she had to be in that graduating class, the winter class. Well, all the names are in there," and he tapped the book. "And the pictures. We can say right off the bat that the girl wasn't in Lois' class, the summer class that graduated in June."

"She couldn't have been," said his wife. "With the baby due in October, it'd have been showing by then, it would have been obvious, everybody in school would have known about it. That's how I know it wasn't Leila. And back then," she smiled a little ruefully, "an illegitimate baby was still something of a disgrace. I think she'd probably have been expelled."

"All right"—and Pryor opened the book—"it had to be a girl in Leila's class, the one that graduated in January. God, this thing brought back some memories. I haven't looked at it in years." He turned the pages slowly, and she peered over his shoulder. "It's funny, as Lois was saying, how you lose touch with people. You've got some good friends in school, you think they'll always be friends, and then you lose touch, go on to other things. Here's Saul Slutzky—he was a hell of a nice fellow—I wonder what became of him. And Tom Murray—we were in the football team together that year— Bill Naylor, I'd forgotten all about him—he was a nice guy too. And Wade Prosser—"

She said, "Oh, wasn't he handsome? A lot of the girls were just crazy about him—he was one of the big men on campus, the big star of the Drama Society."

"Yes, and for all that he was another nice guy," said Pryor. "Not conceited about it at all, just one of the fellows. Looking through this thing gave us both some ideas, brought back a lot of memories."

"Pictures do that better than names sometimes," she said. She took the book from him. "You can almost certainly bet it had to be one of the girls in that class, and probably one of Leila's friends. The way things were then, the teenagers didn't get around as much as they do now, and they were a lot less sophisticated than the kids are now. They weren't as mobile for one thing. Those girls wouldn't have known many other girls, if any, outside of school. And it's a big school, you know. Most of the girls and the fellows would have known a lot of the people on campus by sight, but they all had their own particular sets of friends, the ones they went around with the most. I told you I didn't know Leila Gray at all well, just from having a gym class with her. She had different friends. And looking at all the photographs and thinking back, I can tell you who most of them were. Or were likely to be. She was a very popular girl, she was pretty, and men tend to think that pretty girls can't be friends, but really just the opposite is true—they tend to flock together, at least at that age. Leila went around with the other girls like that, the pretty popular ones who dated quite a lot, and the fellows who were big in athletics or something. I've been remembering which ones. There's Mona Clegg, and Cheryl Shepherd, Pat Fawcett, Barbara Barnhill—" Jesse got out his notebook and pen and began to scrawl the names down. "Eleanor Smithers—and Lucille Fletcher and Ardeth Wickham. Inez Fox and Virginia Lowe. They were all in that set, you could call it, together. Mona Clegg had been going steady with Wade Prosser, most of the other girls envied her like mad, it was supposed to be quite a romance. And she and Leila, and I think a couple of the others, were in the Drama Society. Mona had a big part in the senior class play. Some of the other boys, John Marr and Charles Knapp, were dating some of those girls pretty regularly. There are all the pictures of the senior prom here, and the plays the Drama Society did that year. Goodness, the clothes."

"And they all look so damned young," said Pryor ruefully. "It brings things back, all right. Bill and Tom, I figured them for my closest friends, and Ken O'Neill—I don't think I ever laid eyes on Bill or Tom again after graduation night. The only one in that whole class I've kept up with is Ken O'Neill. He's an LAPD captain downtown now. God, all those years, they just seemed to go by like lightning, and where the hell did they go? It's frightening."

She said soberly, "Yes, it is. At eighteen you think life's going on forever, and then all of a sudden you're sixty and it doesn't seem possible because you feel just the same."

"You think these girls were about Leila's closest friends?" asked Jesse.

"I'd say so. Maybe a couple of others, Beverly Parker, Mary Jane Swanson. I think so."

"And we can have an educated guess," said Jesse, "that Leila wouldn't have gone out of her way to be helpful about the baby for a girl who wasn't a very close friend."

"Well, you wouldn't think so," said Pryor.

"But what I'd like to know," said Jesse plaintively, "is what Leila was doing mixed up in it at all. Presumably all these girls had families. And an illegitimate baby might still have been a disgrace, but I don't suppose any of the families would have been so Victorian as to cast the girl into the night and lock the door on her. Simple discreet thing, the home for unwed mothers, the adoption agency."

"Yes," said Nell, "and another thing, the father was probably one of the boys she'd been dating. In there too," nodding at the book. "From a decent family. The families could have got together and persuaded him to marry her. Only they didn't."

"Maybe the fellow wouldn't have been too keen," said Pryor.

Jesse cocked his head at him. "Because the girl wasn't too particular? You have any memories to share, Mr. Pryor?"

"Oh hell," said Pryor wryly, "you know how fellows that age talk about girls. Just as Lois says, things were different back then. I don't say we were all innocents by any means, but most of it was just talk. I remember—looking at this thing brought back this and that—there were rumors floating around among the fellows that a couple of girls on campus were easy lays. A girl named Kitty McCoy, and another one, Frances Rowan. I've got no idea if it was true or not. Lois and I had been going steady for nearly a year."

She smiled at him. "And all the years I've known you, you never happened to mention that. Rumors get around among girls too, and I'd heard that one. And I'll say something else, Mr. Falkenstein. You just said that Leila wouldn't have gone out of her way to help unless the girl had been a close friend, but I wonder. I knew enough about her, just casually, to know that she was bossy. She liked to be the one to arrange things, and she rather tended to try to order people around. It's possible that she found out about the girl being pregnant, and it needn't have been a close friend, and she remembered me talking about the people who wanted to adopt a baby, and just stepped in. Found out from me who they were, and said to the girl, Here's somebody who might take the baby off your hands."

"Well," said Jesse, "you've given me something to think about, and it's all very helpful. Thanks very much."

Pryor handed him the book. "Keep it as long as you like. It might not narrow it down much—that was a big class—but it would bring you a hell of a lot closer than you are now. I'd say you can be pretty damn positive that the girl was in that class."

She gave a little laugh. "Do you remember when we went to the twentieth reunion, Jim? We missed the tenth one, the first one they held. We had an invitation, but Don was down with the whooping cough. The only one I'd seen since was Betty Jo, and it was a little shock to see some of the others. A lot of them I'd have passed in the street and never recognized—Alice Root had got so enormously fat, and the first boy I ever dated, Leo Stephenson, was already bald. Not everybody was there, not anything like the whole class. I expect some of the boys may have been killed in the war—I never heard."

"Probably," said Pryor thoughtfully. "A lot of us got drafted as soon as we were out of high school—it took a chunk out of our lives. I never got started in law school until three years later. Of course, the first thing you want to get on with is the hunt for Leila Gray. And for all you know, you may locate her with no trouble at all."

"I hope to God I can," said Jesse fervently. "The one I feel sorriest for is the sister, Mrs. Grant. The one Kinsolving thought was his sister."

"Yes." Mrs. Pryor looked a little angry. "All that money he wanted her to have—and committing suicide like that without signing the will."

"And that strikes me as just a little funny," said Pryor. "Of course, people do these things on impulse, but you'd have thought he would have remembered that will. You said he was a damn shrewd businessman. But on the other hand, when he'd reached the age of forty-one without making a will—"

"Yes," said Jesse. "It's the way you said, Mrs. Pryor—it feels as if life's going on forever, and then it catches up to you. Well, I appreciate all the help and advice. Should have asked you before, can't I offer you a drink?"

"Oh, no, thanks, we'd better be going," said Pryor. "It's been very nice meeting you both, and I'll be interested to know how this turns out." He stood up and reached for his wife's arm.

"Nice people," said Nell as she shut the front door after them. "I think I'll go up early and read in bed."

"I'll be up in a while," said Jesse absently. He picked up the book. When she'd gone up, he went out to the kitchen and built himself a bourbon and soda, came back, and sat down with the book on his lap. It was about ten by twelve, the cover of silky faded moire with gold stamping: *Fairfax High School,* and the year. He opened it to find a black and white photograph of the main building of that old school, and on the title page, *Colonial Yearbook.* As he began to look through it, he noticed the pen scrawls on a good many pages, the little memorials the eighteen-year-olds had written in farewell. *Lots of luck always, Mary Ann. Best wishes for happiness in life, Linda. Dear Lois, I've enjoyed knowing you very much, hope we'll always be friends, Alice.* He turned the pages slowly. Class officers, and photographs. Student Council. Girls' Athletic League, Boys' Athletic League, Girls' Service Club, corridor chairmen. Seven pages of winter graduates covered with small close-up photographs. In that year at Fairfax High in central Hollywood, there had been only three black girls and two black boys; the incidence was probably higher now.

For some reason the thing fascinated him. Here were all these people frozen in time, immutable, unchanging. Photographs of the board of education, the teachers. Activities, first semester, and candid shots inset on a number of pages: the variety show, the senior class play, a page of photographs of the senior prom. Close-ups of couples attending: Prosser and Clegg, Naylor and Swanson, O'Neill and Smithers. The Prosser boy had been handsome all right, a young blond Greek god. He turned over more pages. Athletics, first semester, football lettermen. Here was Pryor, and he hadn't changed much in looks, had kept his hair and figure, even if in the photograph the hair was dark and now was gray. Not all of these eighteen-year-olds would have been so lucky, some of them would have got fat, lost their hair, lost their teeth. ROTC, commissioned officers. Basketball team. Girls' athletics—candid shots of girls in shorts playing volleyball, tennis. When he got halfway through the book and came to the section labeled Summer Term he turned back and began to study the individual photographs. These people frozen in time. Some of the girls were pretty, some plain; some of the boys were handsome, some homely; but they all looked so desperately young. Very probably some of these boys had died in the war. He found a photograph of Leila Gray, the formal class photograph. Studying it, he could believe Lois Pryor's estimation of her. She'd been handsome rather than pretty, it was a strong-featured face with a square jaw, rather heavy dark brows, thick dark hair, steady intelligent eyes. The photographs were all black and white, so he couldn't tell about actual coloring. He looked for the photographs of the other girls Lois Pryor had mentioned, and they were all pretty girls, some dark-haired and some blond. Those were the new names to look for now. And something else occurred to him, and he got out his notebook again. In a big school like that, there would have been different classes for the same courses. There were group photographs of all the classes, with lists of surnames below each. It would be a way to sort out which other girls Leila Gray must have known. He went through the pages checking names, and an hour later contemplated the results.

Leila Gray had taken five classes as well as the inevitable physical education class: English literature, chemistry, French, algebra, and American history. There was an average of twenty-six students to a class, about evenly divided between boys and girls. All of the girls Leila had known, according to Lois Pryor, were in one or the other of her classes, and there were twelve or fifteen more. She had been a member of the Drama Society, and so had four of those girls.

He found himself yawning, looked at his watch, and discovered that it was after one o'clock. He let Athelstane out for a last run, ten minutes later let him in again, locked the door and switched off lights and went upstairs. He found Nell sitting up in bed with the light on.

"Thought you'd be asleep a couple of hours ago. You feeling all right?"

"I'm fine," said Nell. "I did go to sleep after I'd finished the book, and then I woke up again. There's something trying to get through to me, and I wish I could think what it is. I have the vague feeling it's something to do with a name. It was— No, it won't come."

"If it's important," he said through another yawn, "it'll come to you sometime." He started to get undressed.

About two o'clock on Tuesday afternoon Clock was typing a report on the new heist that had gone down last night, when one of the detectives from Burglary Division, Hector Romero, came up to his desk. "Say," he said, "I ran into Petrovsky over at the range last night and we got to talking about guns." They all had to keep up a certain standard on the range. "He was mentioning a piece that came into something of yours, a little thing called an Astra. Spanish-made automatic."

"Oh yes," said Clock. "A fellow killed himself with it. In fact, I've still got it here," and he opened the top right drawer of his desk. He had forgotten to hand it over to Jesse. He brought it out and Romero looked at it curiously.

"That's the damnedest-looking peashooter I ever saw. You could tuck it in a vest pocket. Reason I was interested, one like that was part of the loot in a burglary about a month ago, a little more. I'd never heard of the thing. Place down on Romaine. It looked like an amateur job—break-in in the middle of the evening while the people were visiting relatives—and there was the usual mess, the usual stuff taken—tape recorder, camera, portable TV. And the gun. It was an old one, it had belonged to the husband's father. He had the serial numbers on the other stuff, but there wasn't one on the gun. There isn't one on this either. I don't suppose it could be the same gun?"

"Hardly," said Clock. "It's not a common one, but there'll be others around."

"Well, I just wondered," said Romero. "As I say, it looked like an amateur job, maybe a couple of young punks, and he or they wouldn't have known a fence. The loot probably ended up in a pawnshop, and a few of the pawnbrokers aren't as clean as they should be."

"That's so," said Clock, "but that couldn't be connected to our case." Anybody wanting a gun in a hurry could get one under the counter, from the crooked pawnbroker or somebody else, but Kinsolving had been a law-abiding man. He had probably bought this gun legally a long time ago, had never used it, and so it had been there ready to his hand when the sudden impulse hit him in a fit of depression. And yet that nagging little doubt was still at the back of Clock's mind. On the face of it, it had been a typical suicide. That neutron activation analysis—he'd have expected more residue to show, but the lab man had seemed tolerably satisfied. Jesse had dragged his heels on it because of that damned will, but the most commonsensible man on earth would forget all his common sense in a suicidal depression. Anyway, it had been put down officially as suicide and the books were closed on it.

Romero handed the tiny automatic back and said, "I was just curious. You couldn't be sure if it was the same gun anyway, even if it was. How long had your corpse had it?"

"Well, we couldn't be sure about that either, but probably quite a while."

"Oh," said Romero. "Well, thanks for letting me see it." He wandered back to his own area of the big office, and Clock lit a cigarette and scowled at the report in his typewriter. He was thinking about Kinsolving again.

There was that nagging small question at the back of his mind: Had that suicide verdict been right? But there wasn't one damned piece of evidence to say it was wrong. The man had been alone in his apartment, behind a locked door. True, the door had the kind of lock where you could push a button inside to lock it as you went out—or came in. There hadn't been any latent prints in the place except those you'd expect to find—the cleaning woman's, Kinsolving's own. The place hadn't been ransacked, nothing disturbed. His hand had been on the gun when it was fired. And he'd been a quiet man, a man living by routine, a man with only a few friends, and it was very unlikely that anyone had had any reason to want him dead. There couldn't have been any other verdict than suicide.

He stabbed out the cigarette and went back to the report, swearing occasionally at the typewriter.

Jesse had called Garrett on Tuesday morning. "You can call Allen back too. We've got a whole new direction for the hunt."

"He's in San Francisco," said Garrett. "He'll be out of his motel, I probably can't get hold of him until tonight."

"Well, do the best you can," said Jesse. "When he does get back, I want a conference."

"See what I can do," said Garrett. "You're really sticking on this one, aren't you?" He called Jesse at home that night to say he had reached Allen at six o'clock and Allen was getting a late flight down.

"All right, I'll be in your office at nine o'clock."

When he got there, Allen was slouched in a chair looking tired, Garrett puffing at his pipe, Mary Lester her usual slim neat self in a navy dress and low-heeled shoes. Jesse laid the *Colonial Yearbook* on the desk and started telling them about the Pryors, about Leila Gray. "It's a break, as you can see. The first one to look for is the Gray woman, that's priority. If we can drop on her, she might not baulk at all about telling us the girl's name. She might not have seen her in years, even if they'd once been close friends. But I think we've got to take it that it was one of the girls in that graduation class. If we can't locate Gray, then you can start looking for these girls said to have been her nearest friends then. If that's no good, and you ought to be able to find some of them at least, you can start looking for all the ones she had classes with. I made up a list for you."

"You forgot one thing, Mr. Falkenstein," said Allen. "First we check all the names against the birth certificates."

"Oh, by God, yes, of course. That could give us a shortcut, if one of them shows up."

"Fairfax High," said Mary Lester thoughtfully, and opened the book. "Just in that one class there'd have been a lot of girls."

"One hundred and nine," said Jesse. "But you can eliminate the black ones."

"Oh, my God," said Allen.

"But it's narrowed down, and maybe quite a bit, you can see that. You may find Gray right away. Keep me posted. I'll help you out all I can—I can always go to see people evenings and whenever I don't have any other business."

"Back to the marriage licenses," said Mary briskly. "It'd be easier to hunt for a man. And in case she never got married, look in the phone books and directories. Where else? Good heavens"—she'd been looking through the yearbook—"don't they all look so terribly young!"

And Jesse suddenly said, "My God, the class reunion! Mrs. Pryor mentioned it. They had an invitation to the first one, didn't go, they went to the twentieth one. Those things are held every ten years, aren't they? So there must be an alumni association somewhere, and when they send out invitations, they must have a list of names and addresses. That could be a real shortcut. Look, I'm free for the day. There are things I could be doing but they can wait. By God, I wonder if the Pryors would have the alumni association's address. Or the school." He reached for Garrett's phone and found Mrs. Pryor at home. But she hadn't any address for such an association.

"I don't even remember who signed the invitation, I'm sorry. We didn't enjoy it much, it was rather dull, and when we had the invitation to the thirtieth one, we didn't go."

"Well, I'll try the school," said Jesse. "You two can start to look for Leila Gray. If I get anything, I'll check in with Garrett tonight."

But he dropped back to the office first to see if any new business had come in, and just as he came into the anteroom he heard Jean say, "Oh, he's just come in, just a moment, sir." She handed the phone to Jesse. "It's a police officer, a Captain O'Neill."

Jesse said his name, and a deep baritone said, "This is Captain O'Neill down at Narco, Parker Center, Mr. Falkenstein. I was talking to Jim Pryor last night and he was telling me about your troubles. My God, going back to our high school class— I rummaged around and found that yearbook— it made me feel as old as God. But something occurred to me I thought maybe you'd be interested in. That's a funny kind of case you've got."

"Funny isn't the word. What occurred to you?"

"Well, I joined the force three years after I got out of high school, as soon as I got out of the Army after the war. I was a rookie riding a squad car when it happened. I wasn't exactly still wet behind the ears, you could say, but still it rocked me some. I was on the Central beat and I got sent as backup to a ruckus down on Adams, and we picked up a couple of hookers who'd been rolling the johns after slipping them Mickey Finns. And by God, one of them was a girl I'd known in high school. In that graduation class. A girl named Kitty McCoy. I had a couple of classes with her, and I guess you could say I was shocked—well, hell, I was only twenty-two." He laughed. "Well, when I remembered about it in connection with what Jim was saying, I just wondered if she might be the one you're after. I mean, if she went wrong once, she might have gone on going wrong, if you take me. Anyway, I was just curious enough to ask R. and I. about it, and they sent up a package on her just now. We've got a hell of a package on her, Mr. Falkenstein. Prostitution, possession, grand theft, I don't know what all. I thought maybe you'd like to see it—it's on my desk now. And right at the moment she's sitting down in the women's jail waiting for trial on a charge of running a call-girl service. It was her twelfth arrest."

"Oh, thank you so much," said Jesse. "I think I'll postpone what I was about to do and come right down, captain."

CHAPTER SEVEN

Captain Kenneth O'Neill had worn as well as Jim Pryor; he was a big hefty man with a genial expression. There was another man sitting beside his desk in the big office high up in Parker Center, which was LAPD headquarters downtown, and he introduced Lieutenant Gleason of the Vice Bureau. "This was our baby," said Gleason, "she's one of our regulars. Her record goes back before my time. When she got too old for the regular hooking, she started running a stable of girls, sometimes in connection with a couple of pimps, sometimes not, on her own. I ran her down this time. Ken's been telling me why you're interested. If you want to see her, I can take you down."

"Well, it's just possible she could be the woman I'm looking for, I think, and I'd better talk to her. I'd be obliged."

"Sure," said Gleason. He drove Jesse down to the Sybil Brand Institute for Women and talked to one of the wardens. They waited in a tiny cubicle of an interrogation room, and the warden brought in a woman and shut the door. She was a short thin woman with bleached blond hair and a hard poker face; she wouldn't have been bad-looking when she was younger, with a heart-shaped face and large dark eyes, but time and probably liquor had aged her prematurely. "What the hell do you want now?" she asked Gleason.

"This is Mr. Falkenstein. He's a lawyer and he's got some questions to ask you."

"I got a mouthpiece," she said hoarsely.

"You went to Fairfax High School when you were a girl, didn't you?" asked Jesse. "Did you know a girl there named Leila Gray?"

"For God's sake, I don't remember," she said indifferently. "Fairfax High? For God's sake. I didn't go around none with anybody there, school was a drag. I'd've got out and found better things to do, but the old man was so set on education, he was bound I had to graduate, and like a damn fool I wanted to satisfy him. Why the hell are you talking about Fairfax High?"

"One of the girls in that class got pregnant just after you graduated. Would it have been you?"

She stared at him incredulously and started to laugh. "Are you kidding, mister? Me? I was smart enough to stay out of that kind of trouble even back then."

"You don't know what girl it could have been?"

"Like I say, I didn't have much to do with those girls," she said in wry contempt. "All those damn girls looking down their noses at me, on account I didn't have no good clothes, or talked fancy English. I'd gone to Manual Arts the last couple of years, and then Dad got the job in Hollywood and we moved." Her laugh was bitter. "Me having a baby! All those damn girls were pretty stupid, I wouldn't know anything about which one it was. It sure wasn't me. Hell, I was just wasting time in that damned place, and Dad died the month after I graduated—I got off on my own— the old lady was a lush."

Jesse exchanged a glance with Gleason and they both stood up. "It was just a thought," said Jesse sadly in the corridor. "Sorry I wasted your time."

Gleason took him back to his car. He drove back to Hollywood and up to Fairfax High School on Fairfax Avenue. It was a collection of old buildings with the usual spacious grounds, and it wasn't until he'd parked that he remembered suddenly that it was summer vacation and there wouldn't be anybody here.

There was a fellow on a riding mower cutting the lawn in front, and Jesse accosted him. "Would you have any idea where I might get hold of the principal?" he asked.

The man was paunchy and bald, in sweat-stained work clothes. "The principal?" he repeated blankly. "There aren't any teachers here, and won't be till school opens next month."

Jesse went back to the car and found the nearest public phone. He looked up the board of education, wondering if they were all on vacation too, but after a couple of rings a girl answered. "The principal of Fairfax High?" she said briskly. "Well, it's Mr. Haines, but I don't think he's in town. There are the vice principals, the girls' and boys'. Just what did you want, sir?"

"The girls' vice principal," said Jesse. "Can you give me an address for that one?"

"Mrs. Price," said the girl. "I'll have to look it up, just a moment." It was an address in West Hollywood.

He had a little hunt for it. It was an old house on a dead-end street. He thought he'd have known the woman who answered the door was a school-teacher even if he hadn't known who she was; there was an air of brisk authority about her. She was a short plump woman with salt-and-pepper hair, a nondescript round face. She was surprised to see him, hear what he wanted to know.

"Oh no, the school hasn't anything to do with that, the alumni associations. The different classes do that on their own. Usually a couple of the former students get one started. I couldn't tell you anything about that. Which class was it you're interested in?" He told her. "Good heavens, that goes back some way. Before my time." She thought. "Now I'll tell you who just might know something, and that's Miss Rogers. She taught at Fairfax High for nearly fifty years—she only retired twelve years ago. She was always a very popular teacher. Those class reunions." She laughed ruefully. "I had an invitation to one once, and I think it was more out of politeness than a desire for my company. They don't often invite the teachers, you know, only the ones the students really liked and admired. I know Miss Rogers often got invited, she'd mentioned it. She was such a very good teacher, very popular. She was the drama coach for years and years."

"She's retired? Do you know where she's living?"

"Oh yes, we always exchange Christmas cards. Just a moment, I'll get her address for you." She left him waiting on the front porch, came back in a few moments with an address neatly printed on a memo slip. Miss Winifred Rogers, an address in central Hollywood, Russell Street. "She's quite a wonderful old lady, Mr. Falkenstein. She'll be about eighty-five, but still sharp as a tack."

Jesse thanked her. When he found it, it was a little old frame house painted white with green trim, a narrow front porch, a patch of lawn in front. Miss Rogers was very pleased to see him, to have company to talk to, and especially pleased to talk about the school. She invited him into a shabby but very neat and clean living room, asked him to sit down. She was a small thin old lady with a cloud of white hair and an eager wrinkled little face with bright blue eyes behind plastic-framed glasses. "The class reunions?" she said. "Oh, yes, I do like to attend them when I'm asked. It's always interesting to see how the young people have turned out. Which class was it you were interested in?" He told her. "Oh, yes," said Miss Rogers. "That's some time back. Dear me, it would have been a fortieth reunion two years ago if they'd asked me, but I didn't have an invitation. But I do believe I had one for the thirtieth—that was just before I retired—and I always keep everything. I'm a magpie, addresses and such. I'm always pleased to get in touch with the students again, but it doesn't often happen." Her tone was regretful. "A big public school, they leave and put it all behind them. Forget the teachers, and I expect half of what they learned," and the blue eyes twinkled at him. She got up and went across the room to a tall bookcase; after a little search she found what she was after, plucked it out, and came back to her chair. "This is the yearbook for that class." It was the counterpart of Lois Pryor's. She began to look through it. "Oh, yes, that was a good year. You might think, Mr. Falkenstein, that after so many years the young people would be just a blur in my mind, but looking at the faces brings them back as individuals. I've got every single yearbook from my first year at Fairfax. I taught English and speech, but of course the Drama Society was always my greatest interest. I was always interested in the theater and produced most of the plays the classes put on. Of course, I had very able help, from the music directors and the other drama coaches, Mr. Williams and later on Miss Hansen, and the students themselves. From time to time, we had some very talented young people. Oh, yes, I remember this year very well. It was the year we won first place in the one-act play competition at the Pasadena Playhouse, quite an honor since high schools from the whole county were competing. There were some very nice young people in that class." She was studying the photographs page by page. "Mona Clegg took the big female part in the senior play, she was quite good. And Wade Prosser, a very fine type of boy that was, a gentlemanly boy. Pat Fawcett— rather a flighty sort, but such a pretty girl. Lucille Fletcher— Oh, yes, that was a good year. I miss it, you know," she told him. "It was my life for so many years. Since I never married, it was almost as if all the young people were the children I'd never had. But you were asking about an alumni association for this class?"

"Yes, I'm trying to get in touch with some of these people. Do you remember Leila Gray?"

She cocked her head at him like a little bird. "Yes, indeed, she was in the senior play too. A very competent girl, perhaps a little too serious. Now let me see," and she got up again. "I'll have to look in Bill's room. There I go, calling it that when he's been gone four years, but it's habit. We lived together most of our lives, my brother Bill and me. He never married either, and I keep his room for all the odds and ends. I'm a magpie as I say." She was gone for quite a while, and he amused himself by looking through the yearbook again. Presently she came back with a letter in her hand. "I thought probably I had it somewhere," she said. "I will say I have an orderly mind—I keep files on everything. Here we are, the invitation to the thirtieth reunion of that class. "Unfortunately I couldn't attend, because there was a rehearsal for the class play. It was from Regina Coles, but of course her married name is different." She handed it to him. "You can take down the address, but of course it's twelve years ago." He copied it down, an address in San Marino. "I hope I've been of some help, Mr. Falkenstein. And I'm just a nosy old lady, but why are you looking for someone in that class?"

"It's a matter of a legacy," said Jesse. "I'm trying to find the heir to some money."

"Oh, I see." She was enlightened. "How very interesting. Well, I hope this helps you."

"So do I," he said, smiling at her. "You've been very helpful, Miss Rogers, thanks very much." Miss Rogers was indeed a wonderful old lady. He debated what to do with this; it was a little drive to San Marino. Finally he found a public phone and looked in the book. The name, Mandrell, was still listed at the address on the letter. He dialed. "Mrs. Mandrell? My name is Falkenstein, I'm a lawyer looking for some information. It's about your high school graduation class—I understand you're in the alumni association."

"Oh, yes," she said. "At least I was. Why, what's it all about?"

"Well, it's possible you can give me a name and address I'm after. Would it be convenient if I dropped in now?"

"Why, I suppose so," she said rather hesitantly.

"Fine, I'll be there." He got on the Pasadena Freeway; at that hour it wasn't crowded.

The house in San Marino was a low and sprawling stucco, and there was a glimpse of a sparkling pool at one side to the rear. Whatever Mandrell did, there was money here. He thought about all those photographs, the desperately young people; he thought about Kitty McCoy. Some going up and some going down, he thought, and pushed the bell.

She was medium-sized, still with a fairly good figure; she was expensively dressed in a beige sheath, high-heeled sandals. She asked him in reservedly. "I don't know that I can help you much," she said. "We gave up that alumni thing twelve years ago. It was Pat Fawcett and I who started it, that is, she's Mrs. Horton now. It seemed a shame just to lose touch with all your school friends, and we thought it would be fun—interesting—to see them all again, see how they'd changed and what had happened to them. You know. We had quite a time, getting in touch with even some of them. Of course, most of the girls were married and we didn't know their names."

"How did you manage it?" asked Jesse.

"Well, we looked in all the phone books, and we got the *Times* to run a little article about it, asking people to get in touch with me or Pat for tickets, and of course we knew a few of them, were still in touch, and they knew some more." She was thawing a little. "We had a pretty good response, only a fraction of the whole class, of course, but about fifty people showed up, and of course they brought their husbands and wives. So we had a nucleus of the names and addresses to go on with. When it was time for the twentieth, we put an add in the *Times*. We had that at the Wilshire Country Club, and some more people showed up—it was quite successful. Funny to see how people had changed, where they'd got to in life. Neither Pat nor I had been in touch with many of them except Barbara Barnhill. She's the one big success out of that class," said Mrs. Mandrell cheerfully. "She's a very successful writer—does screen plays and TV scripts, of all things. She's absolutely cynical about it, says it's just trash, but she makes a lot of money at it. She never got married at all. But what exactly are you after, Mr. Falkenstein?"

"Names and addresses," he said. "Especially Leila Gray's. Do you remember her?"

"Oh, vaguely. Pat knew her a lot better than I did. I seem to remember she was quite popular in school. But you see, when we arranged the thirtieth reunion, hardly anybody came at all. It was a fiasco, we lost money on it, and we decided to drop the whole thing. People weren't interested after all that time. I was the one who had the list of names and addresses, and I just pitched it out."

"Oh, my God," said Jesse.

"Is it something important? Why are you looking for people from that class? Goodness, I expect some of them could be dead by now. They'd all be around sixty now. The way time goes, it's awful. All that time back— It was during the war, of course, and everybody was overboard with patriotism. Pat and I went out and joined the WACS that April, and I can't say that I regret it—it was an experience—but it's rather funny to think about now. We were both in until the end of the war."

In that case, thought Jesse, neither of them could very well have been the pregnant girl. He felt exasperated. Now if she had been a magpie like Miss Rogers, she'd still have that list, and it would have given them places to look, even twelve years out of date. "What's it all about?" she asked again.

He told her the tale briefly. "You can see that it was probably some girl in that class. Mrs. Pryor thinks it was some close friend of Leila's, but it needn't have been." She was looking suddenly excited.

"Oh, for heaven's sake," she said. "For heaven's sake! I really think I can tell you who it was, Mr. Falkenstein! It just came back to me while you were telling me all that! I hadn't thought about it for years." She was sitting forward animatedly, her eyes bright and interested. "I told you Pat and I had joined the WACS. Well, we got the notice to report in—after we'd had all the physical examinations and all the red tape was through— and we were going to be sent up to Hamilton Field for basic training. So we thought we'd have one last good time together, and we went out to lunch and a movie the day before we had to report. That was about the middle of May. We went to the Roosevelt Hotel in Hollywood for lunch, and it was when we came out and were walking up to the bus stop on Hollywood Boulevard that we saw her. Diane Jessup."

"One of the girls from the class?" asked Jesse.

"That's right. Neither of us knew her well. I'd had an English class with her. And she was obviously pregnant, I'd say four or five months along. We both spotted her at the same time—she was just coming out of a store there, and she couldn't help seeing us, and that we'd noticed. For heaven's sake, Diane Jessup!—of all people—and she pretended she hadn't seen us and sort of dived back into the store. Pat and I just couldn't get over it. I know we both wrote some other girls down here to ask if they knew anything about it, and nobody did. They were all just as flabbergasted too. Of course, we forgot about it later, but every once in a while we remembered, and wondered about it. That could have been the girl you're looking for, Mr. Falkenstein. I mean, if she'd got married, even right after graduation, she wouldn't have been that far along, would she? And," added Mrs. Mandrell, "if she'd been engaged before graduation, everybody would have known about it."

"What sort of girl was she?"

"Well, that was just it, why we were surprised. She wasn't very pretty or very bright—she was rather dim. The boys scarcely came flocking around her. Do you think she could be the one you're looking for?"

"Distinct possibility," said Jesse. "I'm glad you remembered it."

She sat back with a sigh. "Honestly, what a thing. I've got to call Pat and tell her, she'll be terribly interested. But how on earth could you ever find her now?"

"Well, we can have a try. Thanks very much, Mrs. Mandrell."

On the way back to Hollywood he ruminated about it. As Lois Pryor had said, things had been different back then, but human nature didn't change much from one generation to the next. Was it unlikely that more than one girl from that class should be expecting an illegitimate baby about the same time? Probably not, he concluded. It had been wartime, a lot of soldiers around, and those girls had all been young, a good deal more naive and unsophisticated than the current crop of teenagers. For all he knew, half a dozen or more of the girls from that class might have been pregnant by May. But this was another name to look for. He dropped it off at Garrett's office, and then he went up to Oporto Drive.

In the driveway a boy about thirteen was practicing basketball shots into a basket fixed above the garage door. Shirley Grant opened the door to Jesse and said, "Oh, it's you."

"I've got just one question to ask you, Mrs. Grant."

She let him in without enthusiasm. There was a pretty darkhaired little girl about eleven sitting on the couch reading. "Darling, would you please go to your room a while, I've got to talk privately with this gentleman." The girl vanished silently with one curious look at him. "What is it you want?"

Jesse said gravely, "You know, I'm very sorry about the way this has turned out, Mrs. Grant."

"Are you?" she said, but without much bitterness. "Not nearly as sorry as I am. Oh"—she put a hand to her temple—"I don't mean that the way it sounds, as if it was only the money. I'm only human, and money does matter, but the other part of it is the worst. The part about Bob. Have you any brothers or sisters?"

"One sister."

"Can you imagine how you'd feel if you found out suddenly she wasn't your real sister at all? It was like losing Bob all over again when Aunt Janet told me. At first I felt pretty bitter about Dad and Mother, for keeping it a secret, but I got over that. I can understand that they thought it was the best thing, that we shouldn't know. But it was a shock. But then I came to realize that it couldn't change my feelings for Bob, and why should it? Babies get adopted all the time, and most of them probably have better parents and happier lives than they'd have had with their natural parents. But I know how Bob would feel about his money going to strangers."

"Mrs. Grant, this is probably stupid to ask you, but when your father and mother died, I suppose you went through their belongings. Did you come across anything that surprised you, worried you in any way? I know you didn't find anything definite, such as his birth certificate, or the cat would have been out of the bag then, you'd have known. But perhaps there was a name you didn't know in an old address book, something like that?" It was a rather forlorn hope.

She shook her head. "Dad died four years ago. They were living in an apartment on Kenwood then. They'd cleared out a lot of things when they sold the house, and before that when Dad sold the pharmacy. There wasn't as much room in the apartment. I didn't have to do much sorting out until Mother went a couple of years later. After she died in the hospital, Alan and I went over to the apartment, gave the good clothes away, and sold the furniture. Bob helped. She'd left everything to me, she knew Bob didn't need it, and he'd invested that money for them, what they got from the house. It's not a great amount but something. But there wasn't anything like what you mean there. Just clothes, and albums of old snapshots, and"—her face twisted—"the baby books she'd kept for both of us. Things like that. When they'd kept it a secret, they wouldn't have left anything like that for us to find."

"No, I just wondered."

"Maybe it's just as well we're moving away," she said rather savagely. "There are too many memories in this place—this town. At least we've sold the house—we're just waiting to get through the escrow. Alan had to go up to Santa Barbara early. He said just to let the movers do everything, it's worth the extra cost, but there will still be a lot to do. I'm afraid we won't be able to get up there before the school term starts. It'll be difficult for the children changing in the middle of the term, but it can't be helped."

"I'm sorry to have bothered you," said Jesse.

"It's all right. I know it's your job to look for the real relatives."

"And I'm sorry it happened like this, but yes, it's my job."

When he got into the car, he realized he was hungry and remembered that he hadn't had lunch. He found to his surprise that it was nearly four o'clock, too late to have anything now. He drove out to the office on Wilshire.

"Well, and where have you been all day?" asked Jean. "Mr. Loring called. He wants to add something to his will. And you've got a new client who wants a power of attorney drawn up. The poor man—his name's Anderson—needed somebody sympathetic to talk to. His father's terminally ill in a cancer ward and he's never made a will. Mr. Anderson's a bachelor, there were just the two of them. He says the father'll be able to sign it, so he can get at the bank account and so on. He's a plumber. He's coming in tomorrow. Oh, there aren't any other relatives at all."

"Praise be for small mercies," said Jesse. He sat down at his desk to clear up some paperwork in the hour or so before quitting time. Lying in the middle of the desk blotter was a ledger belonging to De Witt's association; one of the girls would have brought it up to date for the month, for handing back to him. De Witt suffered from the illusion that he kept precise records, but he was all too apt to omit dates and add figures in at the last minute without explanation. If he'd just let his efficient secretary, Miss Duffy, do it, all would be well, but having roped Jesse in as treasurer, he preferred to trust him.

He got through a little of the paperwork and at five o'clock went out to the anteroom with the ledger under his arm. "I'm taking off early. Don't take any more appointments than you have to." If Allen and Mary Lester started turning up any of these names, they'd need some help talking to people. He got into the car again and drove down to Santa Monica Boulevard, where the Western Association for Psychic Research occupied a few office rooms in an old building. As he got out of the car, he dropped his keys into his jacket pocket, and felt a little something else there, and brought it out. It was that anonymous little cheap pin the lab man had found just under the couch in Kinsolving's apartment. He climbed bare stairs to the second floor. Miss Duffy was typing briskly at her desk in the anteroom. She looked up and said, "Mr. De Witt's not here. He's over at UCLA. One of the professors in the Parapsychology Department is interested in the cross correspondences."

"More than I am," said Jesse. "I just came by to drop off the ledger." He went into De Witt's office and found Charles MacDonald browsing at the bookcase.

"Oh, hello, Mr. Falkenstein." MacDonald was a thin dark man with serious dark eyes. He was an electrician working for the city, but he took his psychic gift seriously and donated spare time to the association.

Jesse dropped the ledger on the desk and on impulse said, "Like to try a reading for me?" He fished out the little pin and handed it over.

"Let's see what I might get." MacDonald sat down in the desk chair and shut his eyes, holding the pin between both hands. He was silent for several minutes, and then he said, "It's not a happy thing. Not a happy thing at all. There's a lot of envy and greed and bitterness around it. A wasted life, a wasted life." And after another silence he said suddenly, "Bulls. A bull in a china shop. Bulls and oxen." He sat up. "That's all I get from it. I'm sorry, it doesn't sound like much." Like a good many of MacDonald's messages, it was cryptic, and it meant nothing to Jesse. He filed it away at the back of his mind, thanked MacDonald, and started home.

He found Nell tired and cross. "Your offspring's been running me ragged all day. I wish to goodness I had that much energy." Davy came bouncing up and hurled himself at Jesse.

"Wanna play ball, Daddy! Wanna play catch!"

"Not now, big boy. Daddy wants to sit down and relax."

"Find something to play with quietly, darling, please. He's already had his supper," said Nell, "you'd think that might quiet him down." They got him settled with a toy airplane, but he went on loudly making engine noises until she took him upstairs for a bath. Jesse got himself a drink. He was just going out for a refill when she came back again and announced that she'd sit down in peace with a glass of Dubonnet before dinner. "And I hope to goodness he stays asleep. The girl ought not to be so obstreperous."

"You're so positive. Are you going to give it up for adoption if it's a boy?"

"Oh, don't be silly. I know it's a girl," said Nell.

They had just finished dinner and she was straightening up the kitchen when the phone rang. "I've spotted something for you. I don't know whether it means anything," said Allen. "I'm checking those birth certificates against the new list of names, and it's a damn slow job. And a one-man job. I'm not finished with it yet. Now, these names. The girl's supposed to have been one of Leila Gray's bosom buddies. There's one name, Mona Clegg. Well, among the birth certificates there's a Marcia Clark who had a baby boy born on October 27 of that year at a hospital in San Luis Obispo. The same initials, and you know how people do that, making up a phony name. I thought all along it was possible the girl used a different name. You said, what about her family—they'd probably have seen she was taken care of on the quiet— Yeah, it was still a blot on the family name forty-two years ago. So maybe she had an aunt or something up there, and got out of town to have the baby. She may have meant to hand it over to an adoption agency there, only meanwhile the Gray girl thought about the Kinsolvings."

"It's a little farfetched," said Jesse dubiously. "But I suppose it's possible."

"Mary hasn't found any of the rest of them yet, but it's early."

"Well, I have," and Jesse passed on the new information. He had just left Diane Jessup's name at Garrett's office, and elaborated. "Damn it, if the Mandrell woman had had that list—but it's past praying for now. Those initials—it doesn't really say a damn thing. You'd better check the certificates for L.A. County and not go wandering all over the state imagining things."

"I just happened to notice it."

"And with the number of girls in that class, I'll bet you'll find a lot of other matching initials. Even if it means anything, there's no way to check it. Damn it, the girl's enough of a ghost now, if she was using a phony name, it just means she's vanished beyond locating."

"I just spotted it because the Mona name struck me. It's a pretty name, you don't hear it often."

"Don't get carried away," said Jesse.

On Thursday morning he found himself in the cancer ward of Cedars-Sinai, with an anxious Anderson, and Jean along as a witness and notary, looking at a pitifully old and ill man lying in the hospital bed, gray and emaciated. He was very weak, but his mind was working, and he knew what he was doing. He said to his son faintly, "Sorry—should have made will—long ago."

Anderson patted his shoulder awkwardly. He was a man about fifty, small and dark. "It's okay, Pop," he muttered. "This is just as good."

"Glad—your mother's gone. She'd have hated—put me in the hospital. Don't like it much myself," and he tried to laugh, but only gasped. He was able to read the document and understand it, and a nurse propped him up in the bed. He signed it with a slightly shaking hand, and they got it witnessed and sealed.

"I'm much obliged," said Anderson in the corridor. "I'm afraid he hasn't much time left. I'd better stay with him a while. I guess I just leave this with you?"

"That's right. You can sign on the account now, get at the safety deposit box. Just refer the bank to me and I'll take care of it."

Both he and Jean were silent on the way back to the office, for the sober reminder of mortality.

Late on Friday afternoon Mary Lester found the name of Beverly Parker on an old marriage license. It was dated in October forty-two years ago, to Beverly Parker and William Urqhart. So Beverly Parker hadn't been about to give birth to an illegitimate baby about the same time, presumably, but she might know some names and addresses if she was the same one said to have been a friend of Leila Gray's. Mary found the name listed in the phone book at an address in Tarzana, and called to check. It was the same Beverly Parker.

She certainly wasn't going to drive out to Tarzana at this end of the day, and made an appointment to see her on Saturday morning. Private operatives never could count on civilized days off. On Saturday morning she took the Ventura Freeway out there and found the house, a rather ramshackle old place on a lot largely covered with weeds. Beverly Urqhart, who had been a pert and pretty girl in that school photograph, was fat and friendly, with straggly gray hair and obviously false teeth. She was baby-sitting three noisy young grandchildren. She was intrigued to meet a private detective, listened to the names read out, and said, "Gee, I hadn't thought about any of those girls for years. Funny, you're such good friends in school, and then you sort of drift away. No, we never went to any of the class reunions. I had a notice about the first one, but we couldn't afford the tickets. Inez Fox—she was going on to college, I remember, and so was Cheryl. Goodness, you bring back some old times, Miss Lester." And she said, "Leila Gray. I was real good friends with her all through high school, her and Mona and Lucille Fletcher and Ardeth Wickham. There was kind of a little crowd of us that went around together, dated some of the same fellows. I always felt so sorry for Leila—the rest of us had things so much better. I wonder what she did with herself after school. She was a smart girl—I guess she could have got anywhere she wanted."

"Why did you feel sorry for her?"

"Oh, she hadn't any family of her own at all, see," said Mrs. Urqhart. "Her mother and dad got killed in an accident when she was only about ten, and some social service department in the city took care of her. She'd lived in different foster homes ever since. She didn't like the people she was living with then—they were awfully strict and religious and had a lot of rules. She turned eighteen the month before we graduated, and she said she was going to get off on her own as soon as she could get a job, she wouldn't be a minor anymore and could get away from all the foster homes. She was going to get a job and a place of her own. She thought maybe she and Mona would get a little apartment together, both get jobs."

"Mona Clegg?"

She nodded. "Mona, she was just crazy to get to be an actress—she was just positive she was going to be a famous actress, but I don't suppose she ever did. I never heard of her again. I got engaged to Bill that summer, and we got married in October. Mother and Dad were put out about it because we hadn't known each other long. He was in the Army then, and then I was just too busy to think about getting in touch with any of those girls. I followed Bill around for awhile, different Army bases. Thank God he never got overseas. And then I had Jim—that was our first—and after Bill got out of the Army he had quite a time finding a steady job, but he finally did, and then the twins came along—they were sure a handful—and we lived up in Fresno awhile when Bill was with that construction company. I just lost touch with all those girls. I wonder what happened to them all—it'd be interesting to know. You say you're looking for one of them who might inherit some money. Well, I just wish it was me," and she laughed comfortably. She was simple and open and a little stupid, and obviously she hadn't known anything about the pregnant girl, possibly one of the girls she had known. And she'd never been in touch with any of those school friends since.

Jesse offered to help Nell do the marketing on Saturday afternoon, but she said he'd just be in the way, wandering off and picking up all the wrong brands. She left him to baby-sit Davy, who wanted to play catch in the backyard. When she drove in, he left Davy bouncing his ball and went to help her carry the market bags in. "I hate to have to shop on weekends, it's always so crowded. Those are the things for the freezer, don't take them inside." She followed him into the kitchen with a second bag, and as she came up to the table, she said suddenly, "Oh!" and dropped the bag with a thud on the kitchen table. "Oh, that was it! It just came to me out of the blue. I knew it was a name—the night the Pryors were here, it was one of the names she said, it rang a little bell in my head, but I couldn't think what—but it came to me just now, for no reason. Mona Clegg, that was Monica Seton's real name."

CHAPTER EIGHT

"And who the hell is Monica Seton?"

"Was," said Nell. "She's dead. She was a big star in films, of course I don't remember anything about her pictures—I'd have been about eight when she died."

"It doesn't ring a bell," said Jesse.

"No, I didn't remember her either." Nell was putting groceries away. "But that Clegg name stuck in my mind, and it just surfaced. I do remember vaguely it said that hardly anybody knew that had been her real name."

"What said? Where did you see it?"

"In a book I got at the library. Look, just let me put the rest of this stuff in the freezer and I'll tell you about it." Ten minutes later she came into the living room, where he sat sprawled in the big armchair.

"But for God's sake, Nell," he said, "if Mona Clegg turned into a big movie star, why doesn't anybody know about it? I've talked to people who were in that graduation class. In fact, Mary Lester just called while you were out, she'd found another one of those friends of Leila Gray's. Why aren't they all saying, all excited, one of their classmates got to be a big star?"

"I can't imagine," said Nell, "but I'm sure of the name. It's a rather funny name. In a book—it was a book called *Hollywood Murders*, something like that. It was about Hollywood personalities who were mixed up in crimes, mostly murders."

"And how did Mona Clegg come into it?"

"She was murdered," said Nell. "A pair of burglars broke in and killed her when they found her alone in the house. It wasn't a very interesting murder," said Nell as a connoisseur, "the pair of burglars breaking in and committing murder when they found somebody there. She was living in Beverly Hills, I think."

"Well, that's a queer one," said Jesse. "But I thought you said that nobody knew who Seton really was. The people who'd known her before.

So she really did turn into a famous actress. I'll be damned. Don't you remember the title of the book or the author?"

"Just something about Hollywood crimes. It's funny when you think about it, isn't it? But of course it's probably nothing to do with your business. And nothing says that girl was Mona Clegg—she's just one of the possibilities."

"But there is this new suggestion that she and Leila might have been planning to live together after they got jobs." He passed on what Mary Lester had said on the phone. "It's interesting, apart from the rest of it, to find out what happened to these people, all these kids just starting out in life. Some going up and some going down. Probably some of those boys were killed in the war, or in the Korean war just after. So Mona Clegg went way up. And if she was the girl, and she's now dead, probably that money's going to end up in Sacramento—when she hadn't married or had other children."

"I think it said she'd been married," said Nell, "but I don't remember any children. But it could have been her, when she was one of that Leila girl's best friends."

"I think I could bear to look at that book," said Jesse. "This is a queer twist all right." He stood up. "Think I'll run down to the library and have a look. Check up on you—you could be woolgathering."

"Oh, I'm right about the name," said Nell confidently. "I know that."

"Very funny indeed," said Jesse. "You might come and see I don't kill the offspring or the animals when I back out." He got out his keys.

Athelstane was safely engaged in slumber on the back porch, and Murteza was stalking butterflies in the backyard. Nell corraled Davy while he backed out the Mercedes, and they both waved him goodbye. At the local library, he enlisted the services of a librarian, and after a hunt through a card file she came up with something titled *Famous Crimes of Hollywood*. "Would this be what you're looking for, sir?"

"Don't know," said Jesse. "Take a look." It was a thick book, and he took it to one of the tables and looked at it. It was the work of two editors, and the individual articles were written by different authors. He found the one titled "The Tragedy of Monica Seton" and flipped over the pages to it. It had been written by a John Nichols. Jesse scanned it, skimming rapidly. Nichols had evidently been a reporter covering the story. There was a full-page black and white photograph of Monica Seton, and he studied it interestedly, trying to remember those pictures of Mona Clegg in the yearbook. That girl had been dark, with a rather sharp-featured face. He wouldn't have recognized her for the same woman in this photograph, a voluptuous-looking blonde, hair down to her shoulders and smiling seductively at the camera. It was known to very few people, said Mr. Nichols, that Monica Seton's original name had been Mona Clegg. Studio publicity said that she was born in England, her father in the diplomatic service. Oh, really, thought Jesse. And she had been ambitious to go into ballet, but couldn't afford the training. At the apex of her career she had been violently cut off in her prime, wrote Mr. Nichols. At the time, Jesse had been occasionally going to movies, but like most small boys he had gone for the Westerns and adventure films. By the roster of Monica Seton's pictures, she had been starred in *Romances with a capital R.* By the titles of her films, he could judge the type of thing: sultry historicals, costume adventures. She had been a big name for quite a while. She had married two husbands by the time she died, and that was twenty-two years ago.

As Nell had said, it wasn't a very interesting murder. She had been alone in her Beverly Hills mansion when the two burglars got in, evidently believing the house to be empty, and surprised her. She had ended up strangled. The police had tracked down the burglars by the loot, which had been considerable. Monica Seton, said Mr. Nichols, had a well-known collection of jewelry. Some of it had shown up when the police dropped on a fence, and he had given away the names of the burglars, Juan Espinosa and Mario Garcia. They both had records for burglary and robbery. The evidence on them was unanswerable though they'd both denied the murder, tried to claim that she'd already been dead when they got in. They had both received long prison terms for second-degree murder. And so, concluded Mr. Nichols, ended the brilliant career of that talented and popular actress Monica Seton, at the age of thirty-nine, at the height of her popularity. Jesse grunted and got out his notebook, turning pages back. The body had been found the next morning by her agent, Tod Garstein. Also giving evidence at the trial had been Mr. and Mrs. Wilbur Sawyer, who had visited her that evening. Sawyer was identified as her lawyer. They had dropped in for a drink with her and left around 10 P.M., leaving her in a cheerful frame of mind and looking forward to the start of shooting her new picture. "Well, well," muttered Jesse. Twenty-two years ago. He stared into space for a while. So Mona Clegg had made it right to the top—undoubtedly made a lot of money too. The names of the husbands didn't mean a thing to him: Jonathan Oliver, Whitney Pollard. She had divorced Oliver, and Pollard had been killed in a plane crash a couple of years before she died. It would be more than ironic, if Mona Clegg had been the girl who had borne Robert Kinsolving, if both of them had died by violence, those years apart.

Jesse went out and found a public phone. That book had been published ten years ago. He called the *Times*. "Is a Mr. John Nichols still on your staff?" he asked the girl who answered.

"Mr. Nichols is with the editorial department. I'll transfer you." Another woman answered, and he asked if Nichols was in.

"Yes, sir, he's in conference with Mr. Page. Would you like to leave a message, sir?"

"Do you think he could see me for a few minutes in about an hour? My name's Falkenstein. I'm a lawyer hunting some information he may have."

"I should think so, sir. He should be free by then."

Jesse headed downtown for the *Times* building, and sat in the car in the parking lot thinking about this. Allen and those initials. It wasn't anything like evidence, but there it was. And the woman Mary Lester had talked to had said there'd been some mention of Mona Clegg and Leila Gray taking an apartment together after they'd left high school in January. Leila Gray, growing up in the foster homes, eager to get away on her own. What about the Clegg girl's family? She must have had some—who? That girl positive she'd get to be a famous actress, and she had. Made a lot of money, likely. And then dead at thirty-nine. Life could be a funny proposition. That baby would have been conceived sometime that February by any reckoning. Had Clegg and Gray been already sharing an apartment by then? After a while he got out of the car, went into the building, and took the elevator up to the editorial offices. He asked the receptionist for Mr. Nichols, gave her a card. She went away, came back, and ushered him to the door of an inner office with Nichols' name on it in gold.

Nichols was short and stocky, with heavy jowls like a bloodhound. "Well, what can I do for you, Mr. Falkenstein?" he asked, offering a hand.

"I've just been reading the article you wrote about Monica Seton's murder."

"Oh, yes? Sit down. What about it?" He offered Jesse a cigarette.

"I'm curious to know how you knew her real name. Wouldn't bother you, but I've got a case on hand that maybe she comes into, or could come into. I've been talking to people who knew her in high school, and nobody at all seemed to realize that she'd turned into the famous glamour queen from plain Mona Clegg. Which was peculiar."

"Oh," said Nichols, "is that so? Well, you know how studios used to operate? Dream up the phony background to build up the glamour. A lot of the older stars and some of the current ones took on the more euphonious names."

"How did you know her real one?"

Nichols laughed, leaning back in his desk chair. "That was a little funny. The editors of that potboiler asked me to do a piece on it because I'd covered the story for the paper when it happened. I'd forgotten a lot of the details, so I went down to the morgue and looked up what I'd written at the time. Of course, it was a big front-page story, every reporter in the county flocking around, and the wire boys, and stringers for other sheets, trying to get interviews with the detectives, her agent, everybody she knew. The cops wouldn't let anybody in the house, of course, but I just happened to know one of them working it, Sergeant Nogales. He was something of a publicity hound, liked to see his name in the papers, and I'd obliged him now and then. I caught him just as he came out of the house with her agent, the day after the murder was discovered. He was taking the agent in to make a statement. I chased after them to the car, asking questions. I didn't get much for a story, but the sergeant said in looking through the house they'd found her birth certificate and that was her real name."

"Yes," said Jesse, "but if that was in the papers at the time, why didn't all her old friends see it and find out who she was?"

"It wasn't in the papers," said Nichols. "The agent was there, as I said, and he asked me please not to publish that—she'd detested her name and she'd changed it legally and it didn't matter to anybody, did it? Well, of course, there wasn't any news value in it," and he shrugged. "It didn't matter. I didn't use it, but when I came to write that piece for that book, I figured, hell, it was years back and probably most people had forgotten about her by then, so I put it in."

"Did she have any family showing up at the funeral weeping and wailing?"

"I don't know," said Nichols. "Not obviously, as I recall. Of course, we all covered that, it was a splashy affair up at Forest Lawn, everybody from the studio there—the first husband Oliver—he was the Shakespearean actor, you know, getting on a bit then—and some of the top names in the business were there too. There wasn't anybody identified as a member of the family. Maybe she didn't have anybody. We asked the agent, the studio people, and they just said no comment. But why are you looking back into the dim past, Mr. Falkenstein?"

Jesse told him the story briefly, and he wasn't much interested. "Funny rigmarole," he said. "I wonder if she was that girl, whoever it was the Gray woman knew."

"And we can't seem to lay hands on the Gray woman. Do you know where Seton's money went?"

"No idea. I suppose she left a will, but nothing ever came out about that. By the time that would have been getting settled, we were into the trial, and we were all covering that. It only lasted about a week, and there wasn't much news value in that either," said Nichols. "It was an open-and-shut thing. The two punks both had records, and they were placed on the scene. They put up a show in court, very melodramatic, claiming she'd been dead when they got in, they hadn't laid a hand on her, it was two other guys." Nichols shrugged. "It was damned near funny, it was so thin. Some young lawyer from the public defender's office was representing them, but he hadn't a leg to stand on. The whole thing was so obvious it was funny."

"Well." Jesse stood up. "Thanks very much for your time. I wonder if that agent's still around somewhere. Tod Garstein."

"I wouldn't know," said Nichols. "Good luck on your offbeat hunt." He still didn't sound much interested.

Jesse stopped in the lobby to consult the phone book. There was a Garstein and Singer Agency on Sunset Boulevard, and he tried the number but got no answer. He started home, still ruminating. It was all still vague and up in the air, but he was rather liking the idea of Mona Clegg as that pregnant girl. Using the false name to have the baby. Living with Leila Gray? Leila remembering Lois Severson talking about the people who wanted to adopt a baby. Mona Clegg, hellbent to get to the top, be a famous actress. And not wanting to leave a record behind her about the illegitimate baby. It could very well be the answer. Leila Gray parceled out to the foster homes, minus any family, but what about the Clegg girl? If she'd been in the same position, that woman Mary Lester had talked to would have said so. And the Clegg girl's family must have known about the baby. Whatever family. And the lawyer—he hadn't any idea how old the man had been then, he could be dead. But if Clegg had been Robert Kinsolving's natural mother, it was important to find out about the family. How would she have left her money? There must have been quite a lot of money. If it had gone to what family she had, Kinsolving's estate would look like very small potatoes in comparison.

He came into the office a little early on Monday morning, dictated a couple of letters to Jimmy, and was just about to take off when Jean put through a call. "This is Falkenstein."

"Oh, Mr. Falkenstein, this is Patricia Horton. Regina was telling me all about this queer thing you told her about, about Leila Gray and Diane Jessup and all. And when I told her something I remembered, she said I'd better call and tell you."

"Yes, Mrs. Horton? Something about Mona Clegg?"

"Oh, her—no, it was about Leila Gray. Regina said you're particularly interested in finding her."

"I certainly am," said Jesse. "Can you tell me anything about her?"

"Well, I don't know if it would help you at all, it's just a little something I remembered. Regina said I'd better tell you. Regina told you about the class reunions. The second one, the twentieth, was actually more successful than the first, there was quite a good turnout. And Leila came to it. As I say, I'd known her better than Regina had, not as well as some other girls, and I was sorry I didn't have much of a chance to talk to her at that affair. But Regina and I were sort of unofficial hostesses, you know, we were circulating around. Leila came in late, and she was alone. I noticed her coming in. I was talking to Wade Prosser, and he hadn't changed at all, and he was alone too—he said his wife was sick and couldn't come with him. I think I saw him and Leila dancing together later on—we had a three-piece combo in case anyone wanted to dance. Leila hadn't changed much either, I'd have known her anywhere—she didn't look her age, she was always thin, and not a thread of gray in her hair. But I didn't get much chance to talk to her at all, and she left early. The little I did talk to her, I asked if she was married and she said no, not now, so I suppose she was divorced. And it wasn't long after that I saw her going out the door to the lobby, and I went after her and said was she leaving so early, and she said she had to, she was on the night shift and had to get to work. And she went out and that was the last I saw of her."

Jesse repressed a couple of strong words. "She didn't say where she was working?"

"No, nothing, just the night shift. I know it isn't much, but Regina thought you'd like to hear about it."

"Yes, thanks very much," said Jesse. "Do you remember Mona Clegg?" It was unlikely that any of these women shared Nell's interest in the true crime; they wouldn't have come across the book with Mr. Nichols' piece in it and discovered that the old school friend had been metamorphosed into the glamorous screen star.

"Rather vaguely," she said. "Why?"

"Did you know anything about her family?"

"Goodness, no. I suppose she had one, but I don't know anything about it."

"Well, thanks very much for calling, Mrs. Horton." He put the phone down and stood up.

"You've got an appointment at four," Jean reminded him. "Mr. Loring."

"I'll probably be back before then."

He had to hunt for a parking place on Sunset. The public lots were all full, and he had to leave the car on a side street. He walked back to the handsome new office building in the middle of the block. The Garstein and Singer Agency was on the sixth floor. Past a black and gold door he came into a small elegantly appointed anteroom with an expensive-looking blonde sitting at a small desk. "Is Mr. Garstein in?" He gave her a card. "I'd like to see him for a few minutes."

"I'll see, sir." She went away to another black and gold door in the rear wall, presently came back, and held it open for him. He went into a much larger office with a huge mahogany desk facing a wall of windows, and was slightly taken aback at the man who stood up to greet him. He was a dark stocky man in casual sports clothes, and he couldn't be over thirty-five. He surveyed Jesse and said, "You'd make a dandy Lincoln in a costume part. All you need is the beard."

"I've got no ambition to be an actor," said Jesse, annoyed. "I'm looking for a Mr. Tod Garstein. I'm a lawyer, I sent you in a card."

"Oh, yes," and he looked at it. "You want Uncle Tod? Well, he's retired now, retired last year, and just the way we all said, he hasn't got enough to do, he's bored as hell. What's a lawyer want with Uncle Tod?"

"It's about one of his former clients. Monica Seton."

"Oh, really? That was his first big star, and he's never stopped mourning her. You'd better go and see him—he's always pleased to have company. I'll give you the address and phone him to expect you. Oh, he'll be home, he usually is. The only hobby he ever had was golf, and the doctor won't let him play now—he's got a heart condition. It'll make his day to have some company. Aunt Rachel died a couple of years ago, and both his sons live out of state, so he doesn't get to see them often. It was his older brother who started the agency, actually he's my great-uncle—I'm his brother's grandson." He wrote on a memo pad, tore the slip off, and handed it over. "I'll give him a ring."

The address was on Stonewood Drive in Beverly Hills. It was a new

condominium complex, and Garstein was listed on the top floor. Jesse
rode up in the elevator. The apartment door opened a second after he had
rung the bell.

"Ralph called me to say you were coming. Glad to meet you, Mr.
Falkenstein, come in and sit down." The living room was furnished in rich
modern, and he was a contrast to it, a short spare man in old slacks and
sport shirt, with a narrow dark face and bright black eyes. "Tell me what I
can do for you."

They sat in opposite armchairs facing each other, and Jesse said, "It's
about Monica Seton. I'd like to ask—"

"Oh," said Garstein, and the floodgates opened. He looked wistful and
sad and excited all at once. "Now that was quite a girl, Mr. Falkenstein.
Quite a girl. It was nearly forty-two years ago, no, not quite, maybe forty-
one. She was just a kid when she came to me—nineteen, my God. I'd just
been in the business with Joe five or six years. She came to me and right
off I spotted something there—she had what it takes and then some. She
didn't know a hell of a lot, just a green kid, but there was something there
—class and talent. She said all the experience she'd had was in school
plays, my God, but she was a damned good natural actress, and I thought
she was worth taking a gamble on. I talked Joe into it—well, he liked her
too. There were things to do to fix her up, build the image. She had some
two-bit job at a dress shop, and not much money, but I figured she was
worth a gamble. I sent her to have a nose job, not that it was bad but it
could stand some shortening, and got her to a good beauty operator and
turned her into a blonde. God, that made a difference. I talked to Manny
Epworth like a brother, I said, Manny, you're gonna have a great new star
to make you a hell of a lot of dough, and he listened to me. I got her a
contract, piddling to start with but something, and after a while Manny
saw her possibilities and began to build her up. Publicity, the works. The
Monica Seton I'd dreamed up, I thought Mona was too old-fashioned.
But there's a hell of a lot more to it than front, Mr. Falkenstein. It's like
any business—you've got to be willing to work like the devil if you're going
to get any place. And Monica was a good worker. Oh, she was a worker,
that girl. A good girl, and there wasn't any damfool temperament to her
like there is with some. She was good as gold about taking direction, and
ready to sweat ten hours a day if she had to. My God, when they were
shooting *Desert Song*—shooting a picture's no barrel of fun, Mr. Falkenstein—they shot part of it in Arizona, God, it'd get up to a hundred and
twenty on location, it was murder, but Monica worked like hell as long as
the director wanted her on the set, never complained. She was bound

right from the first to be a big star, but she wanted it fair and square because she'd earned it, see? She was a hell of a fine girl. I thought the hell of a lot of Monica. I never got over her getting killed like that. God, I found her, you know. I'd gone to see her about that offer from Paramount —they wanted to borrow her for a picture—and found the front door open—she was on the couch in the living room. Those bastards had strangled her. God. And just by accident, you could say, those two bastards wanting to rob the house. She usually had a live-in housekeeper, but the woman had left and the new one hadn't come in yet. God, she'd have had another ten years before she'd have had to do character work." He was mournful about it. "But she was a friend too—Toddy, she always called me—a fine girl."

"What I wanted to ask about was her family," said Jesse. "Did she have any?"

"Well, she never had any kids. She married Oliver first—he was the Shakespearean actor, you know—he must have been thirty years older. He'd had three or four wives, but he was loaded, and I've got to say Monica had an eye for the money. Well, she'd never had much of anything—you can understand it. When she dumped Oliver, she got that other one on the string, that Pollard. He was in a big brokerage firm back East. It was one of those blue-blood families older than God. He used to like her to spend half the year in New York, and she didn't like it. I figure she'd have dumped him pretty soon, but he got killed in that crash, and who knows who she'd've got on the string next, but that was just the year before she got killed."

"There'd have been a bundle of money," said Jesse.

"Oh, my God, say it twice. She made a lot from her pictures, and she got a hefty settlement out of Oliver, and Pollard left her another pile. I don't know just how much it would have been, but in the millions."

"Her own family," said Jesse. "Who were they? Her parents alive then?"

"Only her mother. That was why she had never had much. Her father died when she was just a kid and the mother had to support them doing whatever she could get. There was a sister, but they got along like two strange bulldogs. Monica never said much about her. She was fond enough of her mother, I guess, but she never saw much of her after she hit the big time. She was busy, it was a different world."

"Was her mother still alive when Miss Seton was killed?"

"Now that I don't know," said Garstein. "She wasn't at the funeral anyway. Like I say, Monica never talked about her. I'm pretty sure she didn't go to see her much. Knowing Monica, I wouldn't doubt she sent her money, saw she was taken care of all right, but I got the impression the mother wouldn't exactly fit in to her new lifestyle. No, I've got no idea where she lived."

"How did the money get left?"

"Now that I don't know either. It wasn't any of my business. Like I say, Monica was smart. She was smart enough to know she didn't know beans about handling that kind of money, and she hooked herself up to some of these brokers who do know, got her into a lot of blue-chip investments. I don't know anything about how she left it, except that she left me a hundred grand because she was grateful for what I'd done for her. I appreciated it, Mr. Falkenstein, not so much for the money as for the sentiment. The lawyer took care of all that naturally."

"His name was Sawyer?"

"Yes, that's the one. He wasn't very old, but I guess he knew his business. He'd just married a coming starlet when the murder happened. He was one of those young men about town, like they say, liked to date the girls in the business."

"Then he may still be around."

Garstein shrugged. "Maybe."

"What about the sister, was she older or younger?"

"Oh, I don't know. Monica never said much about her, just that she was always trying to boss her around, so maybe she was older."

Jesse reflected. Monica Seton would be around sixty if she were still alive. The mother and sister might both be dead. Where the money had ended up, God knew. But if they weren't dead, and Mona Clegg had been the one who had had that baby, the mother and sister must have known about it. He said, "Well, thanks for all the information, Mr. Garstein."

"You haven't told me why you're asking," said Garstein. "She's been dead for twenty-two years, and most people have forgotten her. What's this about?"

"It's a long story." But Garstein had been helpful, and he was a lonely man pleased to have somebody to talk to. He deserved to be entertained. Jesse embarked on the story, and Garstein followed him with interest.

"If she ever had a kid, she never mentioned it to me, but of course she wouldn't. But I wonder—I see you're kind of all up in the air about this, Mr. Falkenstein—if her doctor might have known."

"Do you know who he was? Did she go to doctors much?"

"Hardly at all. She was healthy as a horse, and she took good care of herself. She wasn't an idiot like some of them are—my God, these young ones using pot and coke and booze, some of them did back then too, but not Monica. She knew what that could do to her, her face and figure, and she wasn't about to damage what had got her where she was. But once in a while, like anybody, she'd go to a doctor for a flu shot or something. It was Dr. Thomas Valentine. A lot of people in the business went to him—he knew how to get along with the temperamental ones. I don't know whether he'd still be alive. It was a long time ago." Garstein sighed gustily. "God, how the time goes. I remember—"

Jesse got away from him with some difficulty; he was pathetically grateful for company. That had taken up most of the morning. He stopped at a coffee shop for a sandwich, and at one o'clock was back in central Hollywood heading for Russell Street.

Miss Rogers opened the door to him with a smile. "You're back again."

"Imposing on your sympathy," said Jesse. "I've got another question for you."

"Come in and sit down."

"You remembered Mona Clegg. Do you remember her sister?" If they'd been living in the same place for a while, in the Fairfax High School district, the sister might have attended that school too.

She wrinkled her brow. "No, I can't say that I do, but of course I'd never have known the whole student body, only the ones in my classes and the Drama Society, in our productions. Was she older or younger?"

"I'd think older."

"Well, we can look at the yearbooks."

"You must be the only one with such a collection. It's what I came back to do."

She twinkled at him, going to fetch the books. "We'll both look. These are the two previous years before Mona was a senior." She took one, he took the other, but there was no Clegg among the student body in either one. They tried two more for the two years before that, and came up blank. But as they started through older ones, suddenly she said, "Here she is." She had been in the graduation class five years before Mona's. He took the book—winter graduates, and the pages of small close-up photographs. Halfway down the first page was the name Harriet Clegg. She hadn't had any of Mona's good looks. And of course, Mona's good looks had been changed, what with the nose job and the change in hair color, and it wasn't too surprising that none of her former friends, even seeing her on the screen, had recognized her. This girl hadn't any pretensions to good looks at all. She had a long thin face, a narrow little mouth, small eyes, flat eyebrows and lank-looking hair. He thought that she must have resented her sister's beauty, been envious of her success. No wonder they hadn't got along. She'd have been about five years older then. Around sixty-five now. "Well, it tells me something," he said.

There hadn't been a smell of Leila Gray in all the records yet. She might have vanished into the blue. Now they would start looking for Harriet Clegg.

Mary Lester was back at the microfilm on Tuesday morning. About ten o'clock she found an old marriage license for Diane Jessup and Bertram Wallace, dated thirty-five years back. She took the names down and sighed, sitting back from the viewer to stretch, taking a needed break. She thought about Diane Jessup, unexpectedly running into the two former schoolmates all those years ago, when she was obviously pregnant, sharing their embarrassment, hurrying away, pretending not to see them. She got up and went out to the lobby. Of course, it was a common name. She looked at all the Wallaces just in the Central book with some dismay. It was better, she decided, to run up the phone bill at the office than spend a fortune in coins. She retrieved her car from the lot and drove back to Garrett Associates.

After an hour of phoning she took a break for lunch and started again. There hadn't been many Bertrams, but a lot of *B*'s, and there were six books to get through. But on the sixth call after she had started again, she said to the woman who answered, "I'm trying to locate a Mrs. Bertram Wallace," and the woman said in a hoarse voice, "Well, she don't use his name now—she's divorced, her name's Diane."

"Would you happen to know if her maiden name was Jessup?"

"Why, yes, it was. Who is this?"

"I'm doing some work for a lawyer. We're trying to locate some of the people from Mrs. Wallace's high school class. Can you tell me where she is?"

"Well, she's at work, of course. We live together and I'm off sick with a cold. She works at the Gold Secretarial Service."

Mary thanked her and looked up the address; it was on Sixth downtown. She thought as she drove of what Mr. Falkenstein had said. All the boys and girls in that high school class so long ago, some going up and some going down in life. That was a very queer thing about the Clegg girl. Mr. Falkenstein had told Mr. Garrett about it last night and he had passed it on this morning. Evidently Diane Jessup was one of those who had gone down, or at least not very far up.

It was an old office building right next to one of the very new ones, and when she found the secretarial service on the ground floor, it didn't look very prosperous. There were four women working at typewriters in a dingy bare office, and a stout woman at a table near the door. She gave Mary a toothy smile. "Can I help you?"

"I'd like to see Mrs. Wallace for a moment. On private business."

The woman bristled. "These are business hours, she's got her work to do."

"Doesn't she have a coffee break?" asked Mary meekly. "I won't keep her long."

While she waited for the woman to decide, she looked at the rest and thought she knew which one was Diane Wallace. A thin dreep of a woman with dyed black hair and a dowdy blue dress and an unhappy expression. She felt very sorry for that woman. She had her own reasons for being interested in this queer case of Mr. Falkenstein's. Thirty-two years ago, when she was sixteen, she had had an illegitimate baby. It had been just one of those things—two silly romantic kids—and of course her parents had been right not to let them get married, though he had wanted to. Neither of them out of school yet, and neither of their families had much money. They'd got her into one of those homes, and she'd finished school a year late; of course everybody at school had suspected. Her mother had never let her forget it. She'd been too young and frightened to stand up to them, but for all these years she had bitterly regretted giving the baby up for adoption. And when she'd got engaged to Harry, she'd felt it was only fair to tell him, and he'd turned his back and walked away. Nobody else had ever proposed to her.

The woman came back with the other one in tow, the one she'd picked out. "You may take ten minutes," she said coldly.

"What do you want to see me about?" asked Diane Wallace.

"Could we go somewhere private?"

"I don't know where. There's a bench in the hall."

They sat on the hard bench. When Mr. Falkenstein had given them her name, Allen had found the birth certificate. The baby had been born in the French Hospital on October 27, forty-two years ago. Mary told her what they were looking for, told her they had seen the birth certificate. "You see, it's important to know what happened to your baby, in case it's the one we're looking for. The man left some money, and any blood relatives might inherit it."

"Oh," said Mrs. Wallace. She wouldn't know anything about the niceties of the law.

"What did happen to the baby? Did you give it up for adoption?"

She said dispiritedly, "I had an awful time then. He was a soldier, I didn't even know his unit, and he wouldn't have married me anyway. You were supposed to be nice to soldiers in wartime. I never saw him again. My dad, he kicked me out and I didn't hardly know where to turn." She gave Mary a sideways glance. "You mean if it's my baby you're looking for, there'd be some money in it for me?"

"Maybe."

"Oh. Well, my aunt took me in and— Who got the baby you're looking for, to bring it up?"

"Just some people who wanted a baby. Someone knew the girl and took the baby."

"Well, I guess that could maybe have been my baby then. My aunt knew some people who wanted a baby and they took it."

"What was their name?"

"Oh, it's so long ago I forgot. If you said what it was, I'd remember."

"Would it have been Sherwood?" asked Mary easily.

"Oh, yeah, that was it. I remember now."

Mary stood up. "Thanks for your time," she said dryly. "I'm not so easily fooled, Mrs. Wallace. What really did happen to the baby?"

She looked up sullenly, hit by another disappointment in life. "I gave it up for adoption. I never even knew which it was."

The firm was listed as Sawyer and Klein, at an address in Beverly Hills. Jesse called the number as he waited for a new client to show up, and was answered by a crisply professional voice. "Sawyer and Klein, good afternoon."

Jesse introduced himself. "I'd like to see Mr. Sawyer. It's about a case of my own and he may have some information I need."

"I'm sorry, sir, Mr. Sawyer's very busy. If you want to see him, you'll have to make an appointment. I could fit you in at ten on Wednesday morning or five o'clock on Thursday."

Jesse was annoyed. Evidently no professional courtesy here, all business. He looked at his calendar. He had appointments himself at both times. He told her so. "I'm not even certain that this is the Mr. Sawyer I need to talk to. If I could have three minutes with him—"

"I'm sorry, sir, Mr. Sawyer is with a client. I can put you down for ten o'clock on Friday."

Somewhat grudgingly, Jesse agreed to that. He'd have a bet that Sawyer was one of those smooth talkers, always immaculate in expensive tailoring, catering exclusively to clients with important money. He put down the phone and Jean brought in his new client, a timid-looking woman named Fellows, who wanted to make a will.

She looked at him anxiously, perched in the chair beside his desk. "I've never done such a thing before, because I never had any money to leave anybody—I just work for a company cleans offices, don't make much. But of course, Mother left me the house when she died, and the lawyer that wrote that will, he's dead now. It's not much of a house, it's awful old, and I couldn't believe my ears when the man said how much they'd give for it —a hundred thousand dollars. It's the city—they don't want the house, but they want to build a new freeway ramp right there. I already signed the papers. I suppose I'd better put it in a savings account, but when I was telling Mr. Forman about it—he's my boss—he said I'd better make a will. I've just got my niece to leave it to. Her mother died when she was born, and my brother Tom—that was her dad—he got drowned out fishing."

Jesse picked up his pen. "We'll find something to put it in that yields more interest, Miss Fellows. Now just let me have your niece's name."

Gil Allen, having nearly finished comparing the names of those high school girls with the birth certificates and finding no other match, had switched over to the list of those girls' names, and on Wednesday he located Mary Jane Swanson. She had married a man named Wharton thirty-seven years ago, and the seventh name in the phone book he tried turned her up, in Arcadia. He drove out there to talk to her, and she was a talker. Without once asking why he wanted to know, she spouted information at him, most of it irrelevant. But he learned that in September forty-two years ago she had been attending the University of California at Berkeley, so she hadn't been the pregnant girl. He asked her if she had kept in contact with any of those other girls said to have been friends of Leila Gray's, and read off the names to her. When he mentioned Ardeth Wickham, she said, "Oh, didn't you know about that? It was terrible. I just cried and cried—why, she was only twenty! We'd started college at the same time, at Berkeley the same semester, and it was just the next year, in February, she was killed in an accident. It was just awful—the fellow she was on a date with had been drinking and lost control of the car —"

Allen sighed. He was feeling discouraged about this job.

CHAPTER NINE

Clock had just come in from some legwork on Thursday afternoon. The heat was building up again, and it was murder out on the street, and the air-conditioning was a relief. He sat down at his desk, and a minute later Hector Romero came up. "Say, have you still got that funny little gun?"

Clock looked up. "Yes, why?"

"You won't believe it, but we've picked up those burglars. They'd just got rid of some loot, and one of our street contacts snitched on them. When we brought them in, they came apart without much trouble. They're just small-time punks and they were annoyed at the pawnbroker for shortchanging them. You remember there was that gun reported missing among the loot on that other job. We had the serial numbers on some other stuff missing and found a couple of pieces in that pawnshop—the tape recorder and a camera—but the gun wasn't there. I thought it might refresh his memory to look at one like it."

Clock found the little gun and handed it over, and then suddenly stood up and said, "Mind if I sit in?"

Romero was a trifle surprised. "The more the merrier," he said. In the tiny interrogation room down the hall, another Burglary detective, Kelly, was talking to a little fat dark man across the small table. Romero and Clock sat down on the other side. "That look familiar, Krider? It's a gun just like the one you took in with the rest of the loot from Rodriguez and Fuentes last month, isn't it?"

Krider was looking morose. "Come on, we know you took that parcel of loot off them. Some of it was still there in your brother's pawnshop. He'll be losing his license over it."

"Oh hell," said Krider. "All right, all right. Yeah, so you know about that. So all right. Yeah, there was a fancy little gun like that one. In fact, I guess it could be the same one." He was looking even sadder.

"We identified the serial numbers on that tape recorder and the camera. We know that that gun was part of the loot from the same job. We'd like to know what became of it. It was a gun just like this one, wasn't it? You just said it looked exactly like it."

"Oh, hell," said Krider dejectedly, "all right, it was. I just said so."

"Did you sell it?" asked Kelly.

"Yeah, I sold it. That's what we're in business for, ain't it, to sell stuff? Big deal." He knew he'd be going up for a stretch for receiving stolen property, and Clock didn't need telling that he'd been the route before, he was an old hand at the business.

"Who did you sell it to?" asked Romero.

"I don't know," said Krider instantly. "No, honest, I don't know. For God's sake, so I'm supposed to get the name, check it with the fuzz there's no pedigree, but if I don't sell it, she'd get one someplace else," and he shrugged elaborately.

Romero was a little surprised. "She?"

"Yeah, it was a dame. How should I know her name? Just a dame. She had a lot of blond hair and a lot of makeup. She says she's going off on a trip and she wants a gun for protection. I showed her some and she took a notion to that one right off, said it'd fit right into her purse. She paid me—"

"In cash," said Romero.

"Well, yeah—"

"And you didn't tell her about the waiting period, or ask for her name."

"Nah, it's a nuisance, all the red tape. She paid me and walked out with it."

"What did she look like?" asked Kelly.

"Hell, I don't know, I'm no good at describing people. She wasn't a very young dame, she had a lot of blond hair, and she was plastered with makeup. Just a dame. She didn't know much about guns. I showed her about the safety catch and all."

"Very obliging of you," said Romero. "Was it loaded?"

"Yeah, it was loaded when I took it in. Where'd you get it back all of a sudden? Is that the same gun?"

"Well, is it?" asked Clock.

He peered at it. "God's sake, I don't know. It's one just like it, it could be or it couldn't be."

"Well, let's get you over to jail," said Kelly, "and do some more red tape." Clock and Romero went out after him and the prisoner, and Romero said, "I wonder if it is the same gun."

"It couldn't be," said Clock. "Our corpse had probably had this one for a while."

"A woman," said Romero. "Well, it is the kind of funny little gun a woman might pick. Funny. For protection, and probably if she had to use it, she'd forget about the safety catch. Did she even know she was buying it illegally, under the counter?"

"Not everybody knows how the law reads," said Clock, "about the waiting period. But when Krider asked her for cash—which he did, of course—she must have realized there was something fishy about it."

"Well," said Romero philosophically, "let's just hope she didn't want it to shoot a boyfriend with." He handed back the little automatic and went off after Kelly.

Dr. Thomas Valentine had retired from practice and was probably not far from eighty. Jesse had found him in the phone book, at an address in Beverly Hills, and arranged to see him early this Thursday afternoon. Dr. Valentine was tall and trim, with a small gray Vandyke beard and old-fashioned rimless glasses perched on a high-bridged nose. It was a big gloomy old house. He took Jesse into a huge dark living room, courteously asked how he could help him.

"Maybe you can't," said Jesse. "You may not be practicing any more, but you'll still abide by ethics, doctor, and may not be inclined to talk about patients. But this one's been dead a long time. Monica Seton."

"Oh," said Valentine, and took off his glasses to polish them on his handkerchief. "Yes, what do you want to know?"

"I'd better tell you my interest first," and he outlined the story. Dr. Valentine listened with intelligent interest. His mind was obviously as sharp as it had ever been.

"Monica Seton," he said reminiscently. "Quite an interesting woman, Mr. Falkenstein. I remember her, yes. She didn't come to see me often, and then just for trivial things. She didn't abuse her body with dope or liquor as so many of the theatrical people do. As you say, she's a long while dead, and it's a long time ago. Since it is a legal matter, I don't think ethics enter into it. You want to know whether she ever had had a child. Unfortunately, I can't tell you that definitely," and he put his glasses on again and peered at Jesse over their tops. "I never had occasion to examine her, er, so intimately, shall we say. But I can tell you something, I believe. You may draw the same inference that I did." He was a leisurely old man, not to be hurried. "Now let me think and get it straight in my mind. It came back to me as you were speaking. I did, as her agent told you, have a certain number of the theatrical people as my patients. Perhaps only as a consequence of having my office in Beverly Hills. I might not have planned it that way—they can be difficult, so many of them inclined to what's called temperament." On his tongue it sounded like some obscure disease. "But Miss Seton was not given to that. I should say a very hard-headed woman, a woman who liked money, liked to spend it, enjoyed life and possessed a good deal of common sense. I must think exactly when it was that this occurred." He thought for a full minute. "It must have been at least thirty years ago, perhaps a trifle more. Yes. She came to see me for a pregnancy test."

Jesse sat up. "And was she pregnant?"

"In a very early stage," said Dr. Valentine. "Yes. She was quite upset about it. She didn't want a child. She asked me quite bluntly to abort her, and of course I refused. At the time, it was illegal, as you know. As it still should be, except under certain circumstances. All these irresponsible young people, the abortions on demand—it is deplorable. She seemed a little surprised at my refusal, and she then asked me to tell her where to go for an abortion. I declined to help her and she was most annoyed. Now to the point I wish to make, Mr. Falkenstein. She said, and I quote her exactly, I'll never go through that again. I never heard any more of the matter, but," he added dryly, "she never had the child, or it would have been announced in the newspapers at the time."

"Either she found an abortionist or induced a miscarriage," said Jesse.

Dr. Valentine said even more dryly, "A miscarriage isn't so easily induced. Babies can be stubborn about getting born, Mr. Falkenstein. I don't recall that she ever came to see me again professionally. Of course, she was a very healthy woman with small occasion to visit a doctor frequently."

"Yes," said Jesse, "but that is very damned suggestive, isn't it? She'd never go through that again."

"It certainly seems to say," said Valentine precisely, "that she had had a child. It's not, of course, evidence in a legal sense."

"It's damn close to it," said Jesse. "Thanks very much, doctor. If we can just locate this Gray female, she can tell us definitely."

"One would think, with all the government interference in our lives these days," said Valentine, "that it would be difficult for any person to avoid leaving records behind."

"One would think," said Jesse sardonically. "Well, I'm much obliged, doctor, this is something to think about."

On the way back to the office he thought about it and liked it. It was very damned suggestive indeed. If this said, as it seemed to, that Mona Clegg had had a child, there wasn't much time for her to have had it between the time she left high school and the time Garstein took her under his wing, at the age of nineteen. And Robert Kinsolving hadn't been the only bastard child born to one of the girls in that high school class—they knew about the Jessup girl and there could have been others—another of Leila Gray's close friends. This wasn't evidence, but the implications were interesting.

On Thursday afternoon Mary Lester was feeling dogged about this long tedious job. The introduction of Monica Seton into it was interesting, but didn't really say anything at all. Leila Gray had had other close friends. It could have been any girl in that whole damned class, she thought wearily. The marriage license hadn't shown up for Gray, and between them she and Allen had called every Gray in all the phone books without result. Which wasn't at all strange when you came to think that there were a lot of places in the world besides Los Angeles County. The Gray girl could have gone anywhere. But people usually retained at least a couple of early friends, and if they could locate one, she might know where Gray was now. Allen hadn't quite finished the comparison of names from the yearbook with the birth certificates, and Mary took up where he'd left off. Presently she found a match. In that graduating class there had been a Margaret O'Rourke, and she had had a gym class with Leila Gray. And among the birth certificates was that of a baby born to Margaret O'Rourke, aged nineteen, that November first, at a hospital in Riverside. There was a father's name given, Patrick O'Rourke, but of course as Allen said, the girl might have claimed a husband. Mary went back to the marriage licenses, turned up nothing, and started to look in the phone book. The microfilm had taken the rest of Thursday and it was now Friday morning. Almost at once she found Margaret O'Rourke listed at an address in West Hollywood, and wearily dialed. A smart female voice said, "Dr. O'Rourke's residence."

"May I speak to Mrs. O'Rourke?"

"Dr. O'Rourke will be in her office now," said the voice, emphasizing the title. "Will you leave a message?"

"Where is her office?"

"You'll find her listed in the yellow pages under psychiatry."

Well, for the Lord's sake, said Mary to herself. Some of them going up and some going down. She looked at the yellow pages, and there was O'Rourke, at the Central Clinic, Psychiatry and Neurology, on Hollywood Boulevard. It wasn't far from Garrett Associates. She drove up there, found a slot in a public lot, and went into the usual neat waiting room, with artificial plants and a uniformed nurse behind a high counter. "Is Dr. O'Rourke in?"

"Would you like to make an appointment, madam?"

"No, thanks. I'd appreciate it if you'd just take my card in to her."

The nurse took it. "The doctor's with a patient and I can't interrupt her. It may be a few minutes."

"I'll wait," said Mary. There was nobody else in the waiting room.

Fifteen minutes later the door beside the counter opened and a woman came in; she was a tall woman with broad shoulders, thick short gray hair, a blunt-featured good-humored face just slightly made up. She was dressed in a navy summer suit with a white blouse. "You're Miss Lester? I've got another appointment in twenty minutes, but I must say my curiosity is aroused by a private detective calling on me. What is it you want to see me about?"

"It's about a baby—"

"Sorry, I can't oblige you, I'm the wrong sex."

"I don't mean that," and Mary launched into her tale. "It's just that we've got to know what happened to your baby. We've seen the birth certificate and knew there was one."

Dr. O'Rourke threw back her head and laughed, showing excellent teeth. "Now that's a good one," she said enjoyably. "Me having the bastard child! My God, you're straying back a long way, aren't you? My God, that high school graduation class! I don't think I've laid eyes on any of them from that day to this. No, I didn't go to any of the reunions, think I had an invitation, but I'm not one for harking back to the past out of sentiment." She began to laugh again. "I'm sorry to disappoint you, Miss Lester, but it was some other Margaret O'Rourke had that baby. Let's see, I graduated that January, and that summer I was working at a veterinary hospital to earn some money. Dr. Regis is gone, but Dr. Toomey is still there—he could tell you I certainly wasn't pregnant, and I started premed that fall. Me having the bastard child, that's a rich one!" She was still chuckling when Mary left.

"Oh yes, I can see why you'd want to know," said Wilbur Sawyer. He didn't live up to Jesse's picture of him. He was a tall broad man in a rumpled gray suit, and he had pulled his tie loose, taken off his jacket. His office was expensively furnished, but his desk was a mass of untidy papers. He looked to be in his middle fifties. "That's a very funny story, Falkenstein. Yes, I see all the implications. My wife—my first wife—and I didn't know Monica Seton very well, only in a casual way. Fay had had a bit part in one of her pictures, and when she wanted to make a will, she came to me. I'd just gone into partnership with my father."

"And what was in the will?" asked Jesse.

"Oh, my God," said Sawyer unexpectedly, "how these things can drag on! It's a damned nuisance. I wish the woman would die gracefully and let us wind it up. I'll tell you how it is. Naturally Miss Seton wasn't expecting to die for some time. She was only thirty-two when she made the will. She said she hadn't any relatives but her mother and sister, and she was damned if she'd leave anything to the sister, she'd leave it all to her mother. As you know, it was quite a pile, and she came in for more later on. I pointed out to her that her mother was likely to predecease her, and she just said in that case she'd make another will. She left a hundred thousand to her agent, and I told her it would be advisable to leave a token amount to her sister, so she left her ten thousand. Everything else to the mother, Eloise Clegg. That's it, short and sweet."

"So why is it still dragging on?" asked Jesse.

Sawyer swiveled back and forth in his desk chair restlessly and passed a hand over his thinning dark hair. "Oh, for God's sake, we do have to take some responsibility for our clients, don't we? When she was killed like that—and what a thing that was, Fay and I had seen her the night it happened, you know—I started doing all the red tape. I went to see the mother and sister and told them about the will. They were living together in an apartment in Hollywood. Miss Seton hadn't said anything about it, but I think she'd been giving her mother a regular allowance—it was quite a nice apartment. And I could see after ten minutes that the woman simply wasn't competent to deal with that kind of money—she just didn't understand anything about business. The sister seemed bright enough, but Miss Seton had disliked her intensely, didn't want her to have anything, and I felt bound to abide by that. The mother was in her sixties then. I thought about it and decided to set up a conservatorship. I could have named the sister, but I didn't think Miss Seton would have wanted it that way."

"No," said Jesse, "but after the mother died—if there aren't any other relatives—"

Sawyer gestured helplessly. "I know. But there's nothing I can do about that, is there? I set up the conservatorship—she was quite agreeable to it—it's at the Security Bank where Miss Seton had her account. They've been sitting on it ever since. Paying a monthly allowance to the mother, a pretty hefty one. The other legacies got paid when the will was probated.

And the rest has just been accumulating ever since. A funny thing happened about a year later. The mother came to me and told me it was too much money the bank was paying her, she didn't need all that money to live on, they shouldn't send her so much. The sister was with her and she was looking daggers at her. I don't think there's much love lost between those two. At least it was all tied up so the sister couldn't get her hands on it right away, and that was all I could do."

"Have you got an address for the sister, by the way?"

"I think we've got one somewhere here."

"You mean to say the mother's still alive?"

"Yes, she's about eighty-five and in a convalescent home. I gather she hasn't long to go. And she never made a will." Sawyer sounded vexed. "I pressed her to do so at the time, and she asked me what would happen to the money if she didn't make one, and I had to tell her it would pass to her other daughter as the only blood relative. She just said, all right, that was how she wanted it, so she didn't have to make a will. I had to let it go at that. I'll have Marge look up that address for you, and the one for the convalescent home."

When he came back, Jesse said thoughtfully, "So Harriet will get it all in the end. Miss Seton would have been annoyed about that, wouldn't she?"

"She never expected her mother to get it," said Sawyer. "I think it was a gesture more than anything else—she didn't know who else to leave it to. She'd have expected her mother to die in a few years and then she'd have made another will. Possibly she'd have been married again by that time. Well, of course I get the regular reports from the bank, and they went on paying Mrs. Clegg's monthly stipend up to about two years ago. Then we had a letter from the sister saying that her mother had had to go into a nursing home. I went out with one of the trust officers to check that it was a decent one. For what they charge, it damn well ought to be. And of course, the bank stopped paying into her account, just takes care of all the bills directly, all her expenses. And that's that until the old lady dies, which I gather is imminent."

"And then Harriet gets it," said Jesse. "Well, about my part in it—my possible part—you can see that there's still nothing definite, but if Miss Seton had a baby, the mother and sister probably had to know about it. And very possibly may have known from Leila Gray where the baby went. If it was the baby who went to the Kinsolvings. But there's no way anyone could have known that there was never a legal adoption. And the Gray girl can pin it down for us, if we ever find her. And if that was the baby who turned into Robert Kinsolving, damn it, half of the Seton estate is due to his estate, and Harriet is his blood aunt and she'd end up with the whole kit and caboodle."

The secretary came in with a memo slip and Sawyer handed it over to Jesse. "Thanks, Marge. That's about the size of it. Yes, it seems rather redundant, if that's the word," agreed Sawyer. "But at least when the old lady dies, we can wind it up formally. Naturally if you get definite proof that Kinsolving was Miss Seton's natural child, I'll be interested, and you'll have some red tape to unwind on it too."

"Yes," said Jesse, "and my God, how much has piled up there now?"

"Between six and seven million," said Sawyer with a wintry smile.

"My God, and when I think of it—he'd accumulated quite a nice estate but of course nothing to compare, and when I think of how the Grants would appreciate it, and he wanted them to have it—I feel damned annoyed about this mess. If he'd just signed that damned will before he had the moment's impulse to suicide—"

"Why people do these things only God knows," said Sawyer with a shrug. "And it's certainly made you a hell of a lot of trouble."

"In spades," said Jesse, "and it's not over yet."

But he had had another small idea, and on his way back to the office he dropped in to see Garrett. Garrett was out, but Allen was sitting at his desk brooding over that yearbook. He looked up and asked hopefully, "You got anything new?"

"Maybe," said Jesse. "It just occurred to me, as everybody keeps reminding us, it was wartime. Young people rushing to get married. I understand it's nature's way of compensating for all the young men getting killed in war. And there's a waiting period to get a license in California. Back then, and even now, people who want to get married in a hurry go over to Vegas."

"Now that is a thought," said Allen. "It is indeed."

"And I've got Harriet Clegg's address, but I'll cover it. Even if we never find Gray, I hope Harriet can tell us about the baby."

He had spoken too soon. The address proved to be a shabby old apartment house on Harvard, and no Clegg appeared on the row of mailboxes in the lobby. There was a door labeled Manager and he rang the bell. "Oh, her," said the fat old man who opened the door. "She moved about a year ago. The owners put the rent up and she said she couldn't afford it. She moved."

"Did she leave a forwarding address?"

"Naw, she never got any mail at all. What was the point? I don't know where she moved."

"Do you know where she works? Does she have a job?"

"I suppose so, but I don't know where."

"I'm very anxious to get in touch with her." He handed over a card.

"You're a lawyer, hey? She get left some money? Well, I'll tell you, she wasn't neighborly with anybody in the place that I know of, but she knew some woman lived around here somewhere. When it gets so awful hot, I leave the door open, and I've seen them leaving together, go to a show or something, at night. I don't know her name, but I see her sometimes at the market."

"Well, if you do see her, I'd be obliged if you'd ask whether she knows Miss Clegg's address. Either of you can get in touch with me."

"Okay," said the manager. "I'll keep it in mind."

But, Jesse thought, they would have her address at the convalescent home, as next of kin.

The Falkensteins were going out that night to have dinner with the Clocks. They left Davy with the baby-sitter and got there about six-thirty. Clock was just pulling into the drive. Fran greeted them at the back door. "We can sit down and relax. Everything's in the oven and the salad's all ready, there's nothing to do." But they trooped down to the nursery to admire Miss Elaine, peacefully asleep in her crib.

"Girls are so much easier," said Nell fondly.

Fran laughed. "You haven't heard how she can yell lately. Don't take any bets, Nell."

The hairy black Peke Sally had followed them, and padded back at their heels. Clock brought in drinks and Fran a tray of canapés, and they sat down. Sally leaped into Clock's lap and he pulled her ears. "How's your funny case, Jesse?" asked Fran.

He told them about all the latest developments in detail. "This Seton thing looks very damn suggestive, I think we may narrow it down to that. The mother and sister must have known about the baby, but of course, damn it, there's nothing to prove it was the same baby."

"But it's very funny about Clegg turning into Seton," said Fran, sipping Dubonnet. "And if it hadn't been for Nell, you'd never have known about it. It has sort of opened out, hasn't it? And how funny that nobody knew Clegg was Seton, had got to be a star."

"All that money," said Nell broodingly. "I don't mean hers, I mean

Kinsolving's. It'd just be criminal if it had to go to Harriet, wouldn't it? That poor Mrs. Grant and her family have a sort of moral right to it."

Clock rattled ice cubes in his glass. "It's very peculiar that you should be mentioning the Seton murder, Jesse. It was long before my time, of course, but I was talking to one of the assistant D.A.s the other day and he was mentioning it."

"Oh?" said Jesse. "It's past history, why?"

"Well, I needn't go into details, it's not a very interesting case, but I had to go down there to discuss the evidence—they've decided not to bring a charge—and this and that came up about rules of evidence, and he was talking about some cases where he thought the evidence pointed the wrong way. He mentioned the Seton thing. He was in it. He's the one who defended the killers. Only he doesn't think they were."

"Oh, is that so?" said Jesse.

"His name's Prothero—he was in the public defender's office, just starting out in practice. From what I heard about it from you, it was open and shut, but—"

"Well, it was, Andrew."

"He said that was just the trouble," said Clock. "Refill?"

"Thanks."

"Well, I don't care about that," said Fran as Clock collected glasses, "but I'll tell you, I don't think Kinsolving killed himself. I think he was murdered. Everybody told you he was the last man on earth to commit suicide."

"But nobody had a motive," said Nell. "And there wasn't any sign of a struggle. His family—what he thought was his family—all loved him."

"I don't care," said Fran stubbornly. "He was murdered."

"The scientific evidence," Jesse reminded her. "He fired the gun."

"Oh, science," said Fran, dismissing the whole discipline with one airy wave. "They can be wrong as well as anybody else."

Clock came back with new drinks. "You haven't got even a hint on Leila Gray yet?"

"She could be in Timbuktu," said Jesse. "But we'll get hold of Harriet. Of course, if Mona Clegg had a baby, and I think she did, it needn't have been the one the Kinsolvings got."

"Men!" said Fran. "You are so slow. Of course Kinsolving was Clegg's baby. The times are too tight—you had a glimmering of that, Jesse. She got pregnant just after she graduated from high school, and had it in October sometime, and it was just the next year when she got that agent. She'd had a baby, by what she said to the doctor, and there wasn't any other time she could have had it because from then on she was in the limelight."

"But, Fran," said Nell, "even if she did, there's no proof that it was the baby the Kinsolvings took. There were a lot of girls in that class and the Gray girl knew a lot of them. And at least one of them we know about had an illegitimate baby about the same time—the Jessup girl. There could have been others."

"Very possibly," said Jesse. "Being nice to soldiers in wartime." Fran made a face at him. "Damn it, the Seton thing is suggestive, and especially as there was some talk about her sharing an apartment with Leila Gray, but unless Harriet knows something definite there's no proof at all. I wonder if the mother knew anything, if she could answer questions now. She's in her eighties. But there's Miss Rogers. Some people keep all their marbles up to the end. What are you brooding about?" he asked Clock.

"Well, of course it's nothing at all. That gun." He told them about it.

Fran bounced excitedly in her chair. "Men!" she said again. "There you are, Andrew. Of course it's the same gun the woman bought from the crooked pawnbroker."

"Now look," said Clock. "Kinsolving didn't date women. He wasn't mixed up with any woman at all. He just peacefully sent for the call girl once in a while, and not very often."

"How do you know?" asked Fran. "He could have been leading a double life. Everybody thinking he was so quiet and steady. He could have been mixed up with some woman nobody knew about. And maybe she has a husband or a boyfriend who was jealous."

"Stop romancing, girl," said Clock. "He was sitting quietly on the couch when the gun went off. There was no sign that there was anybody else there. He wasn't the kind of man to go chasing women. And nothing at all connects the gun he was shot with with the gun the burglars got. They were just the same make."

"But I'll bet you he was murdered all the same," said Fran, "even if you never find out about it."

"And another thought just came to me," said Jesse. "Harriet or the mother might not have known a damned thing about the baby, let alone where it ended up. Those initials. It's quite possible that Clegg covered it up from her family, went out of town to have the baby. And may have meant to leave it with an adoption agency, only the bossy efficient Leila Gray stepped in and told her about the Kinsolvings. But it's equally possible that even if Clegg had a baby, Leila didn't know about it, that it was somebody else she knew who had that baby."

Fran said reluctantly, "Oh well, I do see that. But it makes a better story the other way, doesn't it? The glamorous screen star. Oh, well, let's go and have dinner."

On Saturday morning Jesse drove out to the convalescent home where Eloise Clegg was a patient. It looked like a very expensive one, in West Hollywood. He explained to the receptionist, and she said, "I think you'd better see Mrs. Rosenthal. I don't have much contact with the patients." She used the desk phone and presently Mrs. Rosenthal came out, a round cheerful little woman in a white uniform. She listened to what he had to say and shook her head.

"I doubt if she'd be able to answer any questions—her mind's not clear. We're expecting her to go any day."

"Well, in any case, I've got to get in touch with her daughter. I expect you've got her address as next of kin."

"You'll have to ask Linda here. That daughter! I don't think she's been here a dozen times since Mrs. Clegg's been a patient, and asking how she is just hoping to hear she's dead, you can tell. Some relatives are like that —haven't got any time for sick old people. There's another woman comes sometimes, doesn't stay long, and I don't know her name."

But they didn't have an address for Harriet Clegg, only the name of the bank to notify when the old lady died.

"Now I'll tell you," said William Prothero argumentively, "I don't claim to be psychic, for God's sake, but I can size people up as well as anybody." Jesse had found him reading a thick report at his desk in the District Attorney's office, and he'd been glad to be interrupted, have an excuse for some conversation. Jesse was interested in anything about Monica Seton now. "Look, I'd only passed the bar a couple of years before, I wasn't too experienced, but I don't know that I'd have done any more good if I had been. It looked like a plain case to the police, and of course you can see why. There was evidence to put them on the scene, and they both had records."

"Juan Espinosa and Mario Garcia," said Jesse.

Prothero lit a cigarette with a snap of the lighter. "That's right. And damn it, I believed their story, though you may think I was crazy. I thought they were telling the truth, crazy as it sounded. Or maybe not so crazy to anybody who knows the punks. But the police have to go by evidence. I still think they were telling the truth. They were both fairly stupid punks, you know. They said they'd been cruising around Beverly looking for a likely place to hit, and that place was all dark, no lights, and they thought nobody was home. They got in the back door, said it wasn't even bolted. They had flashlights, and they went upstairs looking for the jewelry, the portable value. They picked up a hell of a lot of loot there, the woman was loaded and went in for the diamonds—some of the pieces were custom-made, but the punks wouldn't know about that. They were just on their way out when Garcia wanted to check the front of the house for anything else handy. They went down there, and they were both scared as hell when they spotted her—lying on the couch. They thought she was asleep at first, and then they saw her tongue was sticking out and realized she was dead, and got out fast."

"Strangled," said Jesse. "Not a very usual method for a burglar, is it?"

"Burglars in general," said Prothero, "are shy birds. They seldom go in for the violence. Run like rabbits when they're surprised by the house-holder. Why were the lights all out, as they said they were? She wouldn't have been sitting there in the dark, would she? She was fully dressed—a kind of gold lamé sheath, high-heeled shoes, a good deal of jewelry. If she'd been sitting there reading or something when they came in, their first reaction would have been to run, not attack her. And by the police report it didn't look as if she'd put up a fight. If she'd chased them, which a woman probably wouldn't do, she wouldn't have been found on the couch, obviously killed there—even if one of them had killed her when she chased them, he'd have left her where she fell. But"—he shrugged massively—"they made the mistake of trying to sell that gorgeous identifi-able stuff to an honest pawnbroker. Bingo, the cops picked them up, and they were tied to it. Plain evidence, and who was going to believe that unlikely story from the two stupid young punks who already had the records?"

"You did," said Jesse.

"Look, for God's sake," said Prothero exasperatedly, "I've got no bleed-ing heart, Falkenstein. They were a worthless pair of small-time pro crooks, and what the hell? But I didn't think then and I don't think now that they, or one of them, killed that damned woman. It wasn't in charac-ter."

"What do you think did happen?"

Prothero hunched his shoulders. "Who the hell could guess? The cops had tied up their investigation, were satisfied they'd nabbed the killers. Who knows what happened? Show-business people, they get up to all kinds of antics. You never know what they'll do. Maybe she was two-timing the boyfriend and he found out about it. Or maybe she'd just had a fight with the current one and he lost his temper. It was all cut-and-dried when it was handed to me. I hadn't a hope of getting them off."

"What did they get?"

"There wasn't anything to say which of them might have done it, so they shared the sentence. Fifteen to twenty in Folsom. As I recall, they both served about seven years and got out on parole. It wouldn't surprise me to find out they've both been charged with other counts since then—they were typical pros—but I don't know. You know, Falkenstein, we're all fallible. We can try our damnedest to make the law fair for everybody, but justice doesn't always get done."

"Unfortunately that's so," said Jesse. "It says, *A just weight and balance are the Lord's.* Maybe we can't expect perfect justice on this side of the veil."

Gil Allen called him from Las Vegas at home just as he had wandered into the living room after dinner, Nell busy in the kitchen. "I've got her," said Allen tersely. "That was a little brainstorm you had, about the quickie marriages in Vegas. I've been looking at the microfilm all day, and just before the office closed at six, I found her. Leila Gray. She married a guy named Henry Dietrich forty years back, two years after she got out of high school."

"For the just man falleth seven times and riseth up again," said Jesse gently. "Come on home, and we'll try to find out if she's still here."

CHAPTER TEN

They didn't find her. There were a lot of Dietrichs in all the phone books, and they ran up the phone bill calling them all, and none of them had been Leila Gray.

"She might be a ghost," said Jesse irritably at the end of that. All they had up to now were the fragments, the little bits of knowledge about her, about her working the night shift somewhere twenty-two years ago, that she hadn't changed much since her high school days, bossy efficient Leila, probably divorced, living somewhere in the county then, and if she was living here now, she might have married again. They went back to the marriage licenses, but she didn't show up there.

And Harriet Clegg seemed to have vanished too. She'd moved last year, that manager had said, and she was still listed in the old phone book, and the new ones wouldn't be out for a while.

In something like desperation they were sent back to that second class reunion. Jesse talked to Regina Mandrell and Patricia Horton again. "If you can just remember some of the people who were there—at least a few of their names—I know it's a long time ago, but some of them might give us some lead." At an affair like that it would have been the natural thing for people to talk about themselves, what had happened to them in life generally since those long-ago school days.

They came up with a few names. Tom Murray, Bill Naylor, Evelyn Scott, Mary Fisher, Betty Jo Canning, Doris Durand, Charles Knapp, Linda Adams, Wanda King.

"If you hadn't thrown that list away," said Jesse annoyedly, "we'd have a hell of a lot more to go on."

"I'm sorry," said Mrs. Mandrell humbly, "but how could I have known?"

The men were easier to find, but of course it wasn't as likely that they'd have been talking to any of the women, and would anybody remember after twenty-two years what anybody had said that night?

Betty Jo Canning was very typical, that friend of Lois Pryor's. "I'm sorry," she said, "but I just can't remember anything. I didn't know Leila

very well in school. I talked to her that night, I think, but it was just casual
and of course I can't remember anything she said."

"Well, I suppose it's too much to expect," said Allen, who was talking
to her.

They got some of the same bits and pieces; a couple of people remembered vaguely that in talking to her that night she'd said she was divorced.
Allen found Thomas Murray in his office in a new high-rise building in
Long Beach, in a big architect's office. He was a small sandy man with a
little paunch, and he was surprised at the questions, but cooperative.
"Well, my God, let me think, I don't know that I can tell you much, I
didn't talk to many of the girls that night. Naturally I was more interested
in catching up to the fellows I'd known." He laughed. "My poor wife was
bored stiff, of course, it didn't mean anything to her at all. I was damned
sorry to hear that Bill Wiseman had been killed in the war. I didn't attend
that first reunion or I'd have heard that then. I never saw any service at
all, I got exempted. I never knew that girl you're asking about, the Gray
girl. I was interested to meet Wade Prosser again. I remember I was a
little surprised to hear what he was doing. A lot of us had thought he
might go into show business, he was the big star in the Drama Society, a
damn good actor and a fine singing voice too, but I suppose it's a chancy
business. He said he was in insurance."

Allen suppressed a groan. They had been looking for Prosser so far in
vain, and of course there were those vague mentions that she had been
dancing with Prosser that night of the reunion. He might remember
something she had said then. He was in the phone book, at a middle-class
condominium complex in West Hollywood, but the manager of the place
thought he must be away on a trip, hadn't seen him in a couple of
months, the monthly maintenance fee got paid by a lawyer or a bank. He
hadn't known where Prosser worked. Allen had said, "Well, when you get
the next check, would you mind putting down the address and letting me
know about it? It's important that I get in touch with him." Now, he
thought, they'd start calling all the insurance agencies in the county, and
there were a thousand and one of them.

So far, there hadn't been a smell of the Gray woman. Allen was convinced that she had moved out of the area—she could be in New York or
Indiana or Timbuktu.

It was a week later when Jesse was proofreading a contract that Jean
relayed a call to him. He said his name into the phone, and a male voice

said, "You were here the other day asking about Miss Clegg. The one that moved."

"Oh, yes," said Jesse.

"I told you she knew this woman in the neighborhood, I'd see them go out together, and I'd see that woman at the market. Well, I happened to be there this morning and I saw her, and I remembered you asking. I up and asked her if she knew about Miss Clegg, where she'd moved, and I told her some lawyer'd been asking, maybe it was important."

"Did you get her address?" asked Jesse.

"Yeah, I got her to write it down." He read it off, an address on Spaulding in Hollywood. Jesse thanked him.

Probably the woman was still working, and he wasn't sure when she'd be home. The woman at the market hadn't included a phone number.

After dinner that night he left Nell reading a novel for a change and drove down there, hoping for the solid evidence. It was a small old apartment building on that old street, and Clegg was listed at a rear unit upstairs. He climbed the slightly rickety stairs and found the right door. After seeing that old photograph in the yearbook, he could have predicted what Harriet Clegg would look like now. She was tall and thin, the narrow mouth had turned narrower, and there were deep lines marking her cheeks. Her gray hair was uncompromisingly short and straight, her eyes wary behind plastic-framed glasses. She was wearing a shabby ankle-length housecoat. "Yes?" she said in a nasal voice. He showed her a card.

"I've had a little hunt to find you, Miss Clegg." He introduced himself. "I've got a story to tell you and a few questions to ask you. May I come in?"

Somewhat grudgingly, she let him in. There was a white Persian cat curled up on an armchair, and she picked it up and transferred it to her lap, sitting down. "I guess you'd better sit down. What's this all about?"

He began to tell her. When he had finished, she said flatly, "That's impossible. Mona never had a baby. Not then or any other time."

"Can you be sure, Miss Clegg?"

"She was too all-fired to have the big career, too careful of herself to get into any trouble like that," she said bluntly.

"Was she living with you and your mother that year after she graduated from high school?"

"Well, no," she said slowly. "She wanted to get out on her own. She and some girl she knew got an apartment together."

"Would that have been Leila Gray?"

She stroked the cat on her lap and said shortly, "I don't remember. Mona had a lot of friends."

"You could say certainly that you were seeing her during that year and she wasn't pregnant?"

She ran her tongue around her lips thoughtfully. "Well," she said slowly, "if you put it like that, I've got to say I couldn't say it would have been impossible. We didn't see her for a good part of that year. It was about April or May, as I recollect, she'd gotten a job at a drugstore, but about then she called on the phone to say she'd got another job with one of those USO troops, going around entertaining the soldiers, you knew how they did, and she was leaving town. She wasn't much of a one for writing letters, and it wasn't until that November that she came back to Los Angeles. So she could have had a baby. I wouldn't like to think it of Mona. I can't lie to you and say we ever had much love for each other. We weren't the same kind—she was so set on a career in show business." And so pretty, when you were so plain, thought Jesse. "But I wouldn't like to think she'd have been that immoral, and as I say, I'd have reckoned that she'd be too cautious to get herself in trouble. But I can see now it's possible."

"But you don't know for certain, and of course your mother wouldn't have known either." He swore to himself; this left it still up in the air. "I'm sorry, I'd hoped you could tell me something definite."

"Well, I'm sorry too. I see you'd like to know for sure, but that's all I can say. If she did have a baby, I never knew about it, or Mother. It was after she came back that year that she got herself an agent and he got her into pictures starting the next year or so. I wouldn't have known her the first time I saw her after she'd had the plastic surgery and dyed her hair blond." Her eyes were bitter and scornful. "Just to act in those silly trashy films."

"Well, she was a great success, Miss Clegg, and she made a lot of money."

"That she did," said Harriet Clegg grimly. "And then getting killed like that, her only thirty-nine."

"And you don't remember Leila Gray?"

"Mona had a lot of friends, and they didn't come to the apartment—she'd be out with them. I will say Mona was always considerate of Mother. Mother had a job as a waitress at a big restaurant, and she'd be awfully tired after a day's work."

Jesse stood up. "I'm sorry to have taken up your time, and all for nothing, Miss Clegg."

She put the cat down and went to the door with him. "I wasn't doing anything, just cleaning up the kitchen. I'm sorry I can't help you."

That Friday afternoon Allen found Charles Knapp, who was in the executive offices of a large savings and loan company. He was a tall lean man with gray hair carefully brushed over a bald spot. He was rather annoyed at being interrupted. He thought back to that class reunion impatiently, said it was his wife who had wanted to attend it, he hadn't been much interested. "She was in that class too, you know."

"What was her maiden name?"

"Inez Fox. I suppose she might remember something about it, I don't know. You could ask her—she was going to be home all day." Allen was annoyed in turn. Of course, he'd already been to the house, to ask where Knapp worked; if he'd known the woman was one of those other friends of Leila's, he would have questioned her then. He went back to the address, which was in Altadena, and talked to her.

It had been interesting in a way to see how all these people had worn with time, from those photographs in that yearbook. Mrs. Knapp had worn very well, a spritely little woman with blond-tinted hair and a good figure. When she heard his questions, she poured information at him, quite useless. It was funny anybody being interested in that after all this time, but the class reunion, she could just have kicked herself, she was so mad. She'd known Leila Gray very well all through school. She'd had a wonderful time at the reunion, seeing all those old friends, they'd had a ball, and she'd looked for Leila but hadn't seen her. It wasn't until Regina had joined her group about ten o'clock and said Leila had had to leave early that she had known she was there at all. "I'd just have loved to see her again, and I never knew she was there! Well, there was quite a crowd. And Regina said she'd come in late so I missed her, and then she left early. I was so sorry about it."

So was Allen. This one was pushy and persistent. If she'd talked to Leila Dietrich that night, she'd probably have had some information to pass on —where she was working then, or where she was living. Even twenty-two years out of date, it would have been something to go on.

Fran left the pleasant old house on Hillcrest Avenue at two-thirty, in plenty of time for her three o'clock appointment with the pediatrician. With Miss Elaine in her carrying crib on the front seat, she got to the doctor's office at ten to three, parked in the lot next to the small building, and went in. It might be the earmark of a doting first-time mother to be so fussy about the regular checkups, but better safe than sorry. On the whole, Elaine was a very good baby. She'd been fussing a bit this morning, but she was settled down now, staring dreamily around her and not uttering a sound.

Fran carried her into the little waiting room, which was empty except for the office receptionist, Mrs. Peterson, behind the glass-fronted window at the counter. "Oh, it'll just be a few minutes, Mrs. Clock."

Fran put the baby down in a chair and idly picked up a magazine. Presently she heard Mrs. Peterson dialing the phone on her desk. About thirty seconds later she snapped to sudden attention.

"No, honestly, Leila, I'm not goofing off, I'm supposed to be on my coffee break. There's only one patient in. Look, can you make it for lunch on Sunday? I haven't seen you in ages. About eleven-thirty, and we'll go to the Tudor Room at the Sheraton. Fine, I'll see you then." The phone clicked down and Fran got up and went over to the counter.

"I do beg your pardon, Mrs. Peterson. I couldn't help overhearing. You were talking to a friend—you don't hear the name Leila very often now—do you mind telling me your friend's other name? I really do have a reason for asking."

Mrs. Peterson looked at her with a rather annoyed expression, but she was trained to be polite to patients.

Jesse had just finished talking to a new client about another divorce when Jimmy put through a call. "It's your sister, Mr. Falkenstein. She says it's a life-and-death matter—she's got to talk to you right away."

Suddenly anxious about the baby, about Clock, he snatched up the phone. "Fran?"

"I've found her, I've got her for you!" said Fran excitedly. "Leila. It was just like fate, honestly! She's a nurse at the Beverly Hills Medical Center, she's on the three-to-eleven shift, and she lives in West Hollywood. She's got a married daughter and two grandchildren, and she's not married. She divorced her husband years ago because he was a drunk. I've got her name and address for you. It was just like fate—"

Jesse sat back in his desk chair and said, "Well, for the love of God! Tell me quick how you pulled the rabbit out of the hat!"

And at the moment, she'd be on duty at the hospital. He called her the next morning, and she agreed to talk to him; he'd only said, on a legal matter.

It was a pleasant neat apartment, and Leila Dietrich was one of those whom time had treated kindly. She was a medium-tall slender woman who didn't look her age. There was only a little gray in her dark hair, her skin smooth and her eyes steady and quiet under the rather heavy brows. He sat opposite her and began to explain, and her eyes widened in surprise. At the end she said slowly, "So he's dead. He was such a cute little baby, and a good baby, the little while I knew him. Yes, of course that was Mona's baby. She was so furious and scared about it, Mr. Falkenstein. And I was fond of Mona, I'd have helped her anyway, but you see, I always thought so much of Mrs. Clegg. She may not be a very brainy woman, but she was always so kind to me. She was about the only person who was kind to me those years—I knew Mona all through junior and senior high school. I go to see her at the convalescent home once in a while, to be sure she's getting good care. She hasn't long to live—she'll go any day."

"When did it happen?" asked Jesse. "Who was the father?"

"Wade Prosser. They'd been going steady all that year. And I thought it was some my fault too," she said, "because I'd gone out on a date that night and left them alone in the apartment." Her tone was rueful. "We'd taken the apartment together as soon as we both got jobs. He was leaving for the Army the next day. When she knew she was pregnant, she was so mad and scared, and she was just furious at him—she refused absolutely to write and tell him. He'd have married her like a shot, you know. She said she wasn't going to let a stupid accident ruin her future career, and she wouldn't tie herself to a husband before she got started."

"Why not an abortion?"

She smiled faintly. "You've got to remember that we were both pretty young. Neither of us knew how to find a doctor who'd do that, and she was scared of that too. She didn't want her mother and sister to know. She said Harriet would be throwing it up to her the rest of their lives. Which she would have. Neither of us had much money. She made up some story for Mrs. Clegg and Harriet, why she was leaving town. We went up to San Luis Obispo on the bus, and we both got jobs as waitresses in a funny little cafe in Pismo Beach. The boss was nice—he gave us an advance on our salaries, so we could get a room. But before we left—she was showing then, but she hadn't seen her mother or Harriet in a month or so—I remembered Lois Severson talking in the cafeteria that day, about those people who wanted a baby. I thought it would be a good place for the baby. I went and saw the people, they were nice people, and they just jumped at it. Mona couldn't work the last three months, but we managed on what I was making. She called herself Marcia Clark. She didn't care anything about the baby, you know. And when he was born, we came back here on the bus and I took him to them. The Kinsolvings."

Jesse drew a long breath. "So now we know," he said.

And she said reflectively, "He turned out to be a good-looking man, didn't he?"

"And how in hell did you know that?" asked Jesse, startled.

"Well, it was rather queer, of course," and she sighed. "Mrs. Kinsolving was in the hospital where I worked a couple of years ago. She was dying. Emphysema and a few other things. And I recognized her."

"After all that time?" asked Jesse incredulously.

"Oh yes, she hadn't changed much except to get older. And she had a distinctive burn scar on her left arm—I'd noticed it when I brought the baby to them. She wasn't my patient, but I'd noticed the name, of course. And the family came to see her, I'd heard them talking out in the hall, about Mother. They named him Robert—I heard them calling him Bob."

"Well, I'll be damned," said Jesse. "The long arm of coincidence."

"Yes, it was queer. And so he committed suicide—that's sad. Mona didn't care a damn about him. She was just furious at Wade—she wanted to be rid of the baby and forget the whole thing. She said she never wanted to see Wade again. She got another job and so did I, but we didn't live together again. About a year later I married Henry, but I found out after a while that he'd never straighten out and stop drinking. Mona had always said she'd pay me back for all I'd done, when she started to make good money. She'd had a few good parts in pictures then—she was on the way. We hadn't seen much of each other since, but I knew where she lived. I didn't like to ask her, but I didn't know where else to go, you see. I was going to divorce Henry, and there was June—my daughter. She was three then. And I knew Mona was starting to make very good money. I had to think ahead. I'd always wanted to go in for nursing, but you have to live in, in a training hospital, and there was June. Well, Mona sent me a check for ten thousand dollars. Not even a note with it. I was grateful. It meant I could go into training. I found a good boarding school where they'd take June even at that age, and I got my training. But"—she was still smiling faintly—"the next time I tried to phone Mona, the number had been changed to an unlisted one. I got the message. She wanted to cut all ties to everything in her past. Maybe it was natural."

"Expectable," said Jesse softly.

"She did have quite a career, didn't she?" she said. "Making all that money. When I think how she'd have hated it all to go to Harriet— Oh, I know about that—I always kept in touch with Mrs. Clegg, and she told me about it after Mona was killed. I never could stand Harriet myself. She's a cold unfeeling woman, and she was always so jealous of Mona. As I say, I go to that convalescent home sometimes to see Mrs. Clegg, and I ran into Harriet there not too long ago. She's so anxious for her mother to die she can hardly stand it, so she can lay her hands on all that money." Suddenly she laughed without much humor. "I don't often lose my temper, but I did that day. You see, I know something about how the law reads. And I knew that those Kinsolvings hadn't been going to adopt the baby legally—they said so. And that day when I ran into Harriet, there she was gloating away, talking about all the money, and I was annoyed. Very damned annoyed, Mr. Falkenstein. And I told her about that. About the baby. Robert Kinsolving. I told her who he was, and how I knew. I said I had half a mind to write and tell him that when Mrs. Clegg died he'd have a claim on half the money. Of course, she was flabbergasted—she'd never known a thing about it, and she was furious. I never liked Harriet, and she'd got my back up—she'd been moaning and groaning as usual, saying what a wasted life she'd had, just the dreary piddling little job working for Bullock's Department Store for over thirty-five years, and I—"

Jesse leaped up as if he'd been stung. "Oh, my God!" he said wildly. "The bulls and the oxen! The bull in the china shop! Oh, my God! Mrs. Dietrich, I'll talk to you again later—" and he ran for the door.

"I'll remind you," said Clock, "of the laws about entrapment." They were walking down the hall.

"On the other hand," said Jesse, "the shock value is worth the risk." He pushed the bell. It was just after eight o'clock.

She opened the door. "I've thought of a few more questions to ask," said Jesse. "This is a colleague of mine. May we come in?"

She let them in reluctantly. They sat down on the couch. The white cat was asleep in a different chair. "Oh, by the way, is this yours?" He held out the little pin on his palm. "I picked it up—" and he gestured vaguely toward the hall.

"Oh," she said, "I didn't know where I'd dropped it. Yes, and wouldn't you think the store could have given out something better for a thirty-fifth anniversary—a cheap thing like that after all the years standing on my feet all day and having to deal with snotty customers!" She laid it on the coffee table. "I suppose it fell off when I was going out or coming in."

"No, Miss Clegg," said Clock gently, "it fell off in Robert Kinsolving's apartment the night you killed him. That's where we found it," and he showed her his badge. "You hadn't known about him for all those years, but Leila Dietrich told you that he was Mona's natural son and when your mother dies he'd be entitled to half of all the money." He took out the Astra automatic and laid it beside the pin. "There's a lot of money, Miss Clegg. Enough for two to share, but you didn't want to share it with anybody, did you? And he didn't know about it, but Leila had threatened to tell him. You decided to take a chance. If he should die before she told him, you gambled that she'd just let it go. You went down to that cheap pawnshop—I think you know how the law reads about the purchase of guns—you were wearing a wig and a lot of make-up, but the pawnbroker remembers you and he'll probably identify you." She was sitting rigidly upright, as still as a stone, and her eyes held nothing but bitterness. "You staged a suicide, and for a while you succeeded. Would you like to tell us how? We'll be taking you down to jail and arresting you, and the warrant will come through tomorrow. Have you anything to say?"

She opened her mouth at last. The bitter lines in her face seemed to have deepened in five minutes. "Mona and Mother between them!" she said vindictively. "They ruined my life! What boy was going to look at me when Mona was around? I never had anything all my life, slaving away at that damned job, and then Mona was killed and left all that money to Mother, and Mother should have died twenty years ago so I could have it! All that money! And then Leila told me about the baby—about him—and he could claim half of it! I was going to enjoy that money—all the things I'd never had—and then I was going to leave it to the Humane Society— the only love I've ever had was from my cats. Yes, you're right, it was a gamble. He was the only one with that name in the phone book, and I found out from the manager that he lived alone. I thought if it looked as if he'd killed himself, if Leila went to tell him and found he was dead, she just wouldn't bother. I just rang the bell and told him I was an old friend of his mother's and I had something that had belonged to her I wanted to give him. He was polite. I sat down on the couch and sort of patted the place beside me and he sat down too. And I reached into my bag and got out the gun. It all went fast, but he put up his hand for the gun and jerked his head, and then it went off. Another half second and he'd have pulled the gun away." Clock let out a breath. So that explained the minimal residue on Kinsolving's hand. His last thought must have been complete astonishment at the attack by a total stranger. "And I wiped off the gun, I know about fingerprints, and I didn't like to touch him but I put his hand around the gun so his fingerprints would be on it. I never thought anybody'd find out anything, suspect anything. It was like you said, a gamble. But nobody can stop me getting all the money, and I can get a good lawyer."

Mrs. Dietrich looked at Jesse with horror in her eyes. "I feel as if it was all my fault, Mr. Falkenstein. If I hadn't told her about him, if she hadn't been so greedy for the money— Well, it's another lesson to me never to say anything on impulse. I did that once before, and I was always sorry for it." Her expression was sad and rueful. "It was at that class reunion you mentioned. I told Wade Prosser about the baby. It had been so long ago, I didn't think he'd care, I didn't think it'd matter. Just a thing that happened. But he was terribly upset."

"Now did you?" said Jesse.

"He didn't know Mona was Monica Seton. He kept saying, Why in God's name didn't she tell me—she hadn't any right not to tell me. It might have happened the day before. I was terribly sorry I'd said anything. Is Harriet in jail?"

"The D.A.'s office is deciding what charge to bring. They may call it second degree," said Jesse.

He called Garrett when he got home. "Did anybody ever locate Wade Prosser?"

"Just this afternoon," said Garrett. "We found the lawyer who's been paying the bills. The poor devil's dying of bone cancer in a convalescent home."

Wade Prosser looked up at Jesse from the hospital bed, his eyes tired and sardonic. There were only vestiges left of the young blond Greek god, and the thin hair was white. He said, "You're twenty-two years late, my friend. I'll be dead before they could bring me to trial. But you're quite right, of course." He looked away, out the window. "It hit me like lightning when Leila told me about that. The baby. My baby. I was in love with Mona and I thought she was in love with me. I thought we were going to be married. I was leaving for the Army. She promised to write to me. She never did. I was overseas until the end of the war, and when I got back, she'd just vanished, I couldn't find her. Her mother had moved and nobody knew where. Well, I wasn't a romantic kid any longer and I got over it." He moved restlessly. "I got married. My wife couldn't have children and she was crazy for a baby. We adopted a boy. Maybe some men can feel the same for an adopted son, but I couldn't, she wouldn't let me. She idolized him, she spoiled the hell out of him, and he got into his first trouble at twelve. But that was later." He was still looking out the window, speaking remotely. "That night, when Leila told me, I can't explain what I felt. A son, my own son, and Mona had kept it a secret, never let me know. I had to find out about him, where he was. It never occurred to me that Leila knew—I thought she meant Mona had just given him up. I had to know what she'd done with him, try to find where he was. I didn't know where she lived, but Leila had mentioned the studio where she worked, and I hung around there. It wasn't for three days that I saw her. She came out driving a big open car. My God, Mona— I had to look twice to see it was her. I followed her in my car and she went to that great big house in Beverly Hills. It was about eight o'clock, and just as I parked, some other people drove up and went in. I had to see her alone. I waited until they left, and I rang the bell. She didn't know me at first, and then she laughed at me. She laughed. I asked why in God's name she hadn't told me then, we'd have got married, and she said all she'd thought about was to get rid of it—she wasn't going to let an unwanted brat stand in the way of her career. My baby. And then she said she didn't know who Leila had given it to and didn't care, it was good riddance. My baby. I don't know what came over me—it was like a red haze in front of my eyes. I just reached for her—and then all of a sudden she was dead." He was silent, and said, "I don't know why I turned out the lights when I left. I didn't want to look at her. I'd loved her once, but I didn't want to look at her." He looked up at Jesse. "And then I never could find Leila again. Leila knew where the baby was, and I couldn't find her. I didn't know her married name, and that alumni association didn't have an address. She'd told me she'd seen a little story in the paper about the reunion and just taken a chance on getting a ticket at the door." His thin hand plucked at the blanket. "The boy kept getting into trouble," he said suddenly, "and she wouldn't let anybody discipline him—my wife. She put him between us—he was all she cared about. She finally divorced me." He looked back at Jesse, and small humor crept into his eyes. "Are you going to do anything about it?" he asked.

Jesse stood up. "There wouldn't be much point in it now, would there, Mr. Prosser?"

And out in the corridor he thought, Old sins casting long shadows. And there wasn't much point either in telling Leila Dietrich that she was responsible for that too. He thought about the curious meshes of fate, tying people together in strange ways.

And he must remember to give that yearbook back to the Pryors.

It was the day after that, and he'd just finished talking to a new client when Jimmy put a call through to him about three o'clock. "Mr. Falkenstein?" It was Shirley Grant's voice and she sounded upset. "I'm sorry to disturb you, but I've got something here I think you better see right away. Can you come over right now, please?"

"I'll be with you in half an hour."

In the living room of the house on Oporto Drive, it was apparent that the move was in progress. Pictures were down from the walls, curtains from the windows. She was looking disheveled and distraught. She hardly greeted him before she said abruptly, "Come and look at this." All the drawers had been removed from the handsome old roll-top desk, and one of them was lying on its side. "I left it for you to see just as I found it. I only remember that desk being moved once. It belonged to Dad's father, and he gave it to us for a wedding present—Alan had always admired it. The movers are coming tomorrow and I thought I'd start getting things ready for them. And when I took the right top drawer out—" She gestured. "It was fastened to the bottom of the drawer with tape, and I suppose when the desk was moved before, the tape was still all right, nobody looked at the bottom of the drawer, but by now the tape's all dried out and it fell off."

There was a yellow-stained envelope beside the drawer. Patches of tape still clung to it halfheartedly. "Look at it," she said.

Jesse opened the envelope and took out a single sheet of typewriter-sized paper. There were just a few lines of writing on it in a rather shaky but legible handwriting, and he recognized the neat copperplate of Robert Kinsolving's hand. *As I feel I may be about to die, I will make my last will and testament. I want all my possessions to be divided equally among my parents, Joseph and Etta Kinsolving, and my sister Shirley Kinsolving.* Properly it ended, *Signed and sealed this day,* and the date was appended. His signature followed: *Robert John Kinsolving.*

Jesse collapsed against the wall and started to laugh. He laughed until he wept, and straightened up and gasped weakly, " 'Ring down the curtain—the comedy is ended!' My God, what a joke, what a magnificent joke!"

"But why was it hidden away like that? I don't understand."

"What you told us about that one serious illness, when you were all so worried and he was eventually rushed to emergency. It was just after his twenty-first birthday. I'd have a guess that he wrote this just before that. Oh, God, it's the perfect joke—" He wiped his eyes. "He was feeling rotten, probably running a high temperature, and his mind wasn't functioning too clearly. He wrote the will, maybe felt foolish about it afterward, and hid it away—but I'm more inclined to think he put it there right then, taped to the bottom of the drawer, with a vague idea of keeping it in a safe place. Because he'd forgotten it. When he was back to feeling better, he'd forgotten doing it."

"But it can't be a real will," she said. "It isn't typed or anything—"

Jesse started to laugh again. "There are just two states where a holograph will is legal, and California's one of them, Mrs. Grant. Oh, my God, this is priceless. I always have said that God has a sense of humor. It's a perfectly valid will. There'll be a little red tape to unwind, but now you'll get not only his estate but half of Monica Seton's." She just stared at him openmouthed.

Athelstane and Davy were tumbling over each other in the backyard. He came in the back door. Nell was sitting staring into space in the living room. "Oh, you're early," she said abstractedly as he bent to kiss her. "You know, Jesse, I've gone right off Esther—it's too stately a sort of name for a baby. What do you think of Judith?"

Jesse grinned at her. "Have I got a beautiful tale to tell you, and then I've got to call Fran and Andrew. Oh, it's beautiful beyond belief." He started to laugh again, and it was a little while before he pulled himself together to tell her about it.

About the author

Lesley Egan is a pseudonym for a popular, very prolific author of mysteries. Her most recent novels are *Chain of Violence, Crime for Christmas, Little Boy Lost, Random Death,* and *The Miser.*